Invade

Simon Bishop

Contents

Chapter 1

"Hey, Danny," Beau said, sticking his head into my room. I laughed at his bed head, his light brown hair sticking up in all directions. Obviously, he just woke up. He ignored my laughter and threw me the phone. I caught it with no struggle. "Darren's on the phone."

"Okay, thanks cous," I shouted as he walked down the hall. I put the phone to my ear and smiled, "Hello?"

"Hey Danny," Darren replied out of breath, sounding worried.

"What, Darren? You know this is like the third time you called today. I know you miss me and all, but let's face it, you're becoming too overprotective. I'm fine. I'm definitely stronger now. Stop getting your panties in a twist and stop worrying about me. I miss – "

"Shut up," he growled seriously. My mouth snapped shut, knowing what he was about to say was serious.

"Dar, is everything okay?" I said, sitting up on my bed.

I heard a door shut on his end and hushed whispers. "Darren, what's going on?" I asked again, this time screaming as the talking on his end became louder.

"Danny, listen and listen good," he said, getting to a quieter part of the room. "Jarred just got attacked and he's in critical condition. He wants you here. You're his best friend. In fact, all of us need you here. So, I suggest you get packing and take the next flight down here."

This time, I stood up and paced around my room. "What? What happened?" I gasped, pulling a shaky hand through my dark hair. This wall all too much to digest. I started imagining the worst-case scenarios in my head. "Is Jarred okay?"

"We're all not okay," Darren's voice trembled at the end. I clutched the phone tighter, knowing what he was going to say next would top the cake. There was a moment of silence before Darren let out a sob. "Mom's dead."

It took a while to fully understand what he was saying. Finding words to respond to a declaration like that was difficult. I could feel myself slipping into the same numb feeling I felt when my dad died fourteen months earlier. All I could hear were the sounds of Darren's choked sobs and a feminine voice soothing him.

This couldn't be happening! I just talked to my mother a day ago! I enjoyed the sound of her tinkling laughter when I told her that Beau's cooking was a disaster. I enjoyed the lame joke that she shared. The sound of her voice alone was comforting. It made me feel as if I were home.

Now she was gone.

"Danny, we've just been attacked an hour ago. Mom – mom – she took the bullet for me," Darren continued, trying to keep an even tone. "The doctors told me it would be a miracle if she still lived, so I'm assuming that she – that she –"

He couldn't finish his sentence. My heart dropped into my aching stomach. "I'm sorry, Danny. It's my fault again. It's my fault that both of our parents died. I'm so, so – "

At the other end of the phone, I heard the slam of a door and a voice that sounded a whole lot like Jarred's own. He shouted something that was too muffled to decipher.

"What?" Darren asked in shock. He choked and started to cry again. "What? Are you lying to me?"

Jarred's voice sounded clearer now as he responded to Darren's questions.

"Dar," I shouted into the phone, knitting my eyebrows together in worry. "Darren, what the hell is going on?"

I kept yelling his name into the phone, waiting for his response, but all I heard was the door slamming shut again and a different voice coming from the other end. I felt tears well up in my eyes as I recognized the voice.

"Hey, D, your brother went to go check on your mom," Jarred said soothingly as I began to cry. "Calm down, Danny."

"Jarred, w-what's going on?"

"Calm down. Your mom is fine. She's still alive, Danny!" Again, I couldn't find the right words to respond as my shoulders slumped and my eyes shut in relief. I began to smile and cry in happiness and appreciation that my mother was still alive. "Darren went to go check up on her. She made it. The doctor took the wolfsbane-laced bullet out just in time for her quick werewolf healing abilities to kick in. She's fine, Danny. She's just sick and needs to be treated for a couple of weeks."

"Wolfsbane-laced bullet?" I asked in shock remembering the bullets that were found in the guns my dad had stored in his warehouse.

"Oh, Danny, Danny, Danny. You really are a poor wolf. You can't see the hunters that are hidden in the dark?"

I shivered at the memory of his words, the way he tortured Stacey and my mom, and the way he hated my kind with a passion. Everything started to click together now. Once again, I hated myself for being the reason behind all of it. They wanted me and since they couldn't find me, they were physically hurting the ones I loved. They knew they were my weak spot. I couldn't help the sudden surge of anger that ignited in me.

"Jarred, I'm coming home," I declared, feeling the canines itch out of my gums and my wolf moving underneath my tight skin.

"Coming home, Danny?" Jarred whispered. I could hear the shuffling of his feet. "Are you sure that's a great idea? Wes is still hurt about the whole break up and he's still – "

"I'll deal with it. Right now, my mom is my main priority."

"Okay, I'll call you back later to plan it out. Right now, I have to deal with Alpha duties," Jarred said in a rush as I heard the door open on the other end. "Bye, Danny."

"Bye, Jar."

I've kept in touch with Jarred ever since I've left Huntstown. Ever since then, we've still been as close as we were when I was still there. Jarred has and always will be considered a brother to me. He was there when I told him about how I learned to use my hands to heal things. Yes, I was a hand healer, but I haven't perfected it yet. He shared my happiness with me. He was also there when I experienced the most painful heartbreak I had ever experienced five months ago.

My heart constricted again at the memories.

It was the first time I've ever felt my heart literally breaking into a million of pieces. It felt as if a cobra wrapped itself around my chest, squeezing the life out of me as I panted for more air. I remember the piercing screams mixed with the howls of my wolf that emitted from my chest. My body felt like it was on fire. I remember Beau and my other relatives surrounding me as I curled in on myself, willing for the pain to stop. It was an hour later that I stayed on the ground, limp and lifeless with tears running down my cheeks.

My mate had made love to another woman.

Jarred was pissed off and drove down for the weekend to cheer me up. He was about to beat the crap out of Weston when he heard the news, but Jade – Jarred's mate and Weston's sister – stopped the two of them from getting into a fight. Darren had found out and ever since then, ignored Weston's existence. Both Crescent Pack and Stone Pack were mad at Weston for doing what he did. Weston shrugged it off.

I still love him and I guess that was what hurt the most.

Every now and then, I would feel the familiar burn in my chest. It occurred so many times already that my wolf learned to take it lightly and eventually, we both got used to it. She was hurt, but she did not abandon me. If anything, she wanted to help me get stronger. Therefore, she helped dim the pain every time he would make love to another woman.

The memory caused me to touch my Crescent Shaped mark that sat where my neck met my right shoulder. A tear rolled down my cheek. I missed him, but I knew he didn't miss me.

I quickly wiped away my tear when I heard a knock on the door. Beau stuck his head inside, his hazel eyes showed concerned. I knew he wasn't going to leave me alone until I told him what happened.

He was as stubborn as I was.

"Just to let you know, I was eavesdropping," Beau said quietly and sat on the couch in my room. "You already know me - nosy."

Beau Wrode was nineteen - just like me. He hadn't found his mate yet, but he couldn't wait to find her. I knew that whoever his mate was was extremely lucky. He'd treat her like a queen and would cherish her and spoil her.

Beau was a Healer of the Wounded, meaning he could only heal cuts and bruises. He was stronger than I was in many ways – including his senses, agility, and energy. He's been training me ever since we first met and because of him, I was a better Healer now.

"I'm coming with you whether you like it or not," Beau declared.

"I have no problem with that, Beau. There was just one thing. They're not too fond of Healers."

"You mean, the prick isn't too fond of Healers," Beau growled, directing it towards Weston. "I don't care what he thinks, Danny. I just want to be there for Auntie Ella and you. That dickhead doesn't deserve satisfaction."

Beau knew everything about me. That included my heavy past about Huntstown, Michigan. He knew about Warren. He knew about Jarred. He knew about who were supposed to be mated to each other. He knew about my friendship with everyone in Huntstown.

I wasn't overly excited to go back to Huntstown. Reuniting with my friends, my brother, and my mom made me all giddy inside. I missed them so much that I couldn't wait to see them. There was just one thing I wasn't so sure about.

My mate.

He would probably be mad at me for coming home. He'd probably not allow me to be on his territory. Whatever he'd do, I wasn't too happy to see the man that broke my heart and the mate that I thought was perfect. I really don't know where this reunion may lead to, but I was about to find out soon enough.

"Then, you better start packing because we're leaving first thing in the morning," I sighed, grabbing the dusty luggage at the back of my closet.

Chapter 2

AUTHOR'S NOTE: NOT EDITED!

"I completely forgot to ask and I feel like such a bad friend," I spoke with sympathy on the phone. "I can't believe I forgot that Darren told me you were in critical condition. I guess I got distracted when he told me my mom was dead."

"No biggie. I'm fine. Just a few scratches and bruises here and there," Jarred said. "When I was on the phone with you, I was much better. My wolf is such a bad ass that it's helping me heal a lot faster. Where are you at now?"

I grinned and felt the nervousness bubble in my stomach as I passed the old worn out sign that read "Welcome to Huntstown! Home of the mythical forests!" in faded yellow lettering. The wood was damp, green algae covering the legs.

"I just crossed the border," I said happily.

"Just hurry up and get your fine butt over here," Jarred whined. I heard a loud thump and Jarred's grunt. I laughed, assuming it was Jade. "Okay, okay, babe, stop it. You know you're my one and only."

"Oh, Jarred, still the same as ever," I said through the phone. "I'll see you in twenty minutes. Bye."

I finally made it back home and all the emotions were bubbling to the surface. Beau laughed as he rolled down the windows, letting the cool air blow through our hair. I sniffed the familiar green leaves and the scent of both the Crescent and Stone pack mingled in the air.

"I love the wind blowing through my hair!" Beau screamed, catching the attention of a few people as we drove by local restaurants and small stores.

"You're a true dog," I joked. "Maybe that's why Cheryl dumped you for the human."

"And you're a true bitch," Beau grinned. "Plus, that was her mate. Get over that."

"You cried like a baby," I laughed. "I remember how badly hurt your ego was that you went through the whole popular phase. That was funny. Remember how you went up to that one girl and she called you cute for sharing that one pick up line?"

"No," Beau snapped, turning red. He took off his sunglasses, seeing as how it wasn't really sunny this time of year. I could see the memory bouncing in his hazel eyes.

"Is your dad a baker? Because you're a cutie pie," I snorted after I recited the words.

"Oh, shut up," He laughed, ruffling my hair.

"Please slow down with my car, Beau. You know how much I love my Land Rover," I scolded as he turned sharply. I gripped onto the black leather clad seats as he sharply turned another turn.

"Land Rovers aren't all that!" Beau shrugged.

"Just slow down, okay? We don't have to rush to get there. I don't want us to get into an accident," I lied.

Don't get me wrong, I was overly excited to see my friends and family. I wanted to squeeze the living daylights out of them. I also wanted to hug my mom – to feel the comfort of her slender fingers playing with my long brown hair. I wanted to see for myself that my mother and my best friend were all right.

Then there was the other thing that made me want to stall this trip back home. Weston Marshall. How would he react with my return? Did he even know I was coming back? What if he didn't love me anymore or he wholly dismisses the fact that we're even mates? What if he married somebody else and had his babies with her?

The thought clenched my heart. "No," my wolf said. "Don't think that way. He'd never go that far."

Beau sensed the worry in my voice and he looked at me. I'm pretty sure that he could see the conflict swimming in my green eyes. He sighed, slowing down until we were just cruising.

"Danny, you have to face him eventually," Beau said as he clenched the steering wheel so his knuckles were white. I'm surprised the wheel didn't crush under the pressure being applied to it. "I personally can't wait to see his face with bruises on it."

"Beau, I really appreciate that you're looking over me like a normal cousin would do, but please don't cause any trouble with him," I fiddled with the loose thread on my white sweater. "This trip isn't about him. It's about my mom and Jarred."

"I can't stand that he did that to you. A mate is a precious gift and he's lucky he even found his own," Beau said, envy dripping from his voice.

"Promise me you won't?" I pleaded.

"Okay, fine," he huffed.

"You'll find your mate soon," I smiled. "She'd be lucky to have you."

Beau didn't seem so sure of my reassurance, so he simply nodded and shifted in his seat. We didn't say much and the car was silent. It was a comforting silence though as we were too absorbed in our own thoughts to say anything.

I felt the nervousness deep in my belly as we turned into the street with the humongous pack house at the end of the street. It's huge structure could be seen from here with the smoke coming out of the chimney in gray swirls. It was a deep brown color with large windows and balconies.

The Crescent Pack had bought a new pack home, using the old yellow one as a meeting area between them and the Stone Pack. They've decided to purchase a new one for – nothing in particular. They just wanted a new and bigger hang out spot.

Beau pulled into the driveway, parking in front of the huge double doors. I sniffed the air, noticing that the Stone Pack was here as well. The laughter and conversation coming from inside the house died down as the engine from our car cut off.

I wasn't even half way out of the car when the double doors slammed open and familiar dark hair and rusted color hair came running my way. I shrieked when they almost tore off my baby's door and practically squished me to death.

"Danny," Elliot yelled in happiness. "Finally! You know how boring it's been since you've left? I had to endure Abigail and Jade's constant PMS-ing."

"Yeah, you know how hard it was to be in the middle of Abs and Eli's constant banter alone? I missed it when we used to make fun of them," Jet cried in joy. "Now I'm not so alone anymore!"

The two boys let go of me and Eli smacked the back of Jet's rusted hair covered head. I laughed at them and noticed Beau standing off to the side looking quite uncomfortable. It's unfamiliar territory for him so I understood.

"Guys, this is my cousin, Beau," I gestured towards the male standing next to me now. I pointed towards the two males in front of me. "Beau, this is Jet and Eli."

They did a man handshake and started to haul the luggage into the house and up the stairs. I followed behind, hugging my arms to my chest. Sniffing the air, I only found the slight trace of the familiar manly smell that I missed in the time I was gone. My arms slumped in relief and disappointment.

While the boys traveled up the stairs, I stayed behind looking at the pictures of the Crescent Pack that hung on the cream-colored wall. My eyes found a picture of me, smiling as Weston held me tightly from behind as he kissed my cheek. It wasn't on the wall, however. I found it faced down on top of the fireplace. My heart clenched again.

"Sorry about that," I heard a familiar feminine voice say as she took the picture from my hands. She hung it back on its hook on the wall. Her crystal blue eyes showed concern. "I'm still putting pictures on the wall.

We haven't completely settled in yet," Jade lied and gave me a comforting smile.

"You don't have to lie to me, Jade," I said. "But thanks for trying. Plus, you look like you're a clown on crack when you lie."

"When did you get so mean?" Jade laughed and hugged me. I returned the embrace and laughed with her.

"When did you get short hair?" I said, pulling back and playing with the black hair that framed her face in a bob cut.

"Since Eli thought it was funny to bleach half my hair in my sleep," Jade pouted and crossed her arms over her chest.

I laughed at Eli's idiocy and ruffled her hair. "It looks nice. I could never pull off short hair."

Right when I was done saying that, I heard a warrior battle cry. I looked up at the second level, startled and saw Jarred climbing over the banister about to jump on top of me. Before he could crush me, I used my werewolf ability to move out of the way and watched as he landed on his face, groaning.

Jade rolled her eyes and helped him up, "How many times do I have to tell you to stop getting yourself hurt? You're still recovering."

"Gosh, she's gotten super fast," Jarred slowly got up, smoothing out his shirt. "I give you credit for that.

I couldn't respond as I gasped in shock at the bruises on his face. His bare arm was covered in gauze, blood clearly visible. My hands trembled at the sight of Jarred. I've never seen him so wounded and injured. I'm sure my face paled as tears welled up in my eyes at my wounded best friend.

"Jar," I whispered, coming closer and touching a bruise on his face lightly. "What happened?"

"I don't want to kill the welcome home vibe, so you'll just have to wait for the meeting tomorrow to find out what happened," Jarred shrugged it off like it was nothing. He opened his arms and crushed me into his chest. I was momentarily out of breath when I hugged him back.

"I'm glad you're okay," I said, letting go of him and noticing the small smile on Jade's lips. She was happy that her mate reunited with his best friend.

"Of course I'm okay! Nothing could take me down!" Jarred hollered. I rolled my eyes at his cockiness.

"Yeah right," Jade snorted. "I've taken you down before."

"That's right, baby," Jarred continued, putting his arm around her shoulders and nuzzling her neck. "You could take me down anytime."

"Okay, ew. My eyes are burning," I screamed, covering my eyes with my hands.

The couple laughed and settled for just holding hands. I looked down at their linked hands, feeling envious towards their perfect relationship. My wolf howled and I had to remind her it was my fault that we weren't exactly happy right now.

I heard Jet, Beau, and Eli come down the stairs as they talked about the training Beau does on a daily basis. Jet whistled at the amount of work Healers put into their training. Eli looked intimidated, but still praised the hard work and dedication that Beau does.

"At least Abs is not around or else, you'd feel like you were watching porn," Jarred groaned. "I swear, Eli and Abigail have the worst case of public display of affection in the whole nation."

I poked my tongue out in disgust as Eli turned the color of a ripe tomato. "Where is Abs?"

"She went with Stacey to see Warren," Jade said with no elaboration.

I quickly dismissed it with no questions asked. The tense silence that followed lasted a couple of seconds as they all looked at me. I cleared my throat and smiled.

"Guys, this is Beau," I motioned towards my cousin. Jade and Jarred introduced themselves, welcoming him with bright smiles.

"Did you visit your mom and Darren yet," Jarred asked, concerned.

"Not yet," I sighed, scratching the back of my neck. It reminded me of Weston, so I quickly dropped my hand. "I'm going there when Darren calls. They went to the were doctor for a daily check up."

"You're staying here, right?" Jade asked with a warm smile and I nodded.

"My room is being used as an equipment sight for all my mom's medical machines," I said. "I hope its okay that I stayed."

"You're welcomed anytime," Jade said. "In addition, Beta Eli gave you permission."

I was about to say something when I heard the distant sound of car doors shutting. The familiar manly smell wafted up my nose, causing my wolf to jump in joy. I froze, feeling my heart drop into my belly. My heart beat faster with every step that grew louder as he approached the front of the house.

What confused me was the sweet, feminine smell that mixed with his and the heavier sound of footsteps that followed after him. I inhaled deeply, trying to recognize the smell. However, I couldn't. I shrugged it off. It was probably a new werewolf.

Everyone around me watched me with wary eyes. Beau stood behind me as we all awaited the presence of my mate. I really didn't want this moment to come so soon, but I quickly closed my eyes knowing I had to encounter him sometime.

When I opened my eyes, there he was staring back at me with his beautiful crystal blue eyes that darkened like a storm. I could see all the emotions that flickered in them. He opened his mouth to say something, but he was at a loss of words.

He was still as handsome as before with his black hair cut short, his prominent jaw line, his sculpted cheekbones, and his muscled arms I remembered myself being wrapped in. My wolf demanded that I embrace my mate now, but I followed the same muscled arms that used to hold me and saw that his hand was intertwined with a smaller hand.

My world came crashing down as I took in the woman next to Weston. She was around my age and she was extremely pretty. Her light brown hair was in a lose side braid, her shorter hair framing her heart shaped face. She looked happy to see me as her lips pulled into a big, welcoming smile. She was … average. She wasn't a slut like I was expecting to see wrapped around Weston. She was normal and … human.

For a couple of seconds, it was quiet as I wallowed in on myself. I could literally feel my heart breaking in two. My vision started to blur, but I blinked back the tears and plastered on a fake smile. "Hello, Weston," I addressed formally and his expression never changed. He still looked at me with all the emotions flickering on his face. "This is Beau Wrodes, my cousin."

I looked up at Beau to see his lips set in a thin line. His light brown eyes had darkened in anger. "Calm down, Beau. You promised," I spoke through the mind link. He didn't listen, but stared at Weston as if he wanted to kill him right there.

"Baby, are you okay?" The female next to Weston put a hand on his shoulder in worry. I held in the growl that dared to escape my lips.

That seemed to snap Weston out of whatever he was thinking. He ran his hand in his hair before glancing at me again. He, too, plastered on a fake smile as he spoke. "Welcome back, Daniella," I cringed when he said my whole name. His smooth and deep voice brought back memories of when he used to tease me, tell me a story, and whisper adoring words in my ear. I shook it off. "Beau, welcome to Huntstown." Beau shifted his weight, but didn't say anything.

"Uh," Weston continued, still wearing that fake smile. "This is Hayley Price, my - um - my girl friend."

"Nice to meet you," I forced out. "I'll see you guys at dinner. I'm going to go – um – unpack my stuff."

"Do you need help?" Jade asked, her voice soothing. I didn't dare look at anyone else in the room afraid that if I met their sympathetic eyes, I would burst.

"Um, no. Thank you."

Walking past Weston and into the corridor where the stairs were located, I felt the tears roll down my face and heard the whimper of my wolf as she cried too.

Chapter 3

Even if I sat as far away as possible, I was aware of his every movement.

Usually, I would bathe in his manly smell that engulfed me for the past two hours. I would bury myself in my favorite scent, content and happy. However, it felt suffocating when I reminded myself that we weren't together anymore or he didn't want me.

Weston was quiet, occasionally looking in my direction. My wolf would purr every time he secretly glanced at us. My hands itched to wipe the intsy bit of food that smeared on the corner of his mouth. Whenever I was aware that Hayley entwined her hands with his own, I had to stop the growl that wanted to escape from my lips.

"Danny," Jet groaned, smacking his forehead with his hand. "Please tell them to stop!"

I laughed when he motioned towards a bickering Abigail and Eli. They sat across each other, leaning forward in the heat of the moment. Beau, who sat next to Eli, stared at them with wide eyes.

"Listen to me, Elliot Cooper –," Abigail scolded angrily, her face turning red.

"Only if you promise to talk dirty, babe," Eli winked, crossing his arms over his chest. His gray eyes danced with amusement while Abigail's green eyes glared at him.

Abigail twirled a piece of her long blonde hair before biting her lip suggestively. She looked down at Eli's lips. Slowly dragging her gaze to look straight into his eyes, she smiled seductively. I held back my laughter when Eli's eyes widened before darkening.

"Why don't we -," Abigail said sweetly before someone interrupted her again.

"Oh gosh," Jet cried, gripping his hair with both his hands. "Please shoot me now!"

However, the couple ignored his comment.

"Why don't we go to your room," Abigail said suggestively before her voice went harsh. "So that way, I could suffocate you with all your pillows."

"Oh come on," Eli leaned back, still smiling at Abigail. "You know you love me."

"Shut up, lover boy," Abigail said, before returning her gaze towards me. "Where's Jade and Jarred? They sure are taking long with the dessert."

In that precise moment, we heard glass shattering inside the kitchen. We all laughed when Jarred yelled, "Ouch! Gosh, Jade, it was an accident!"

"That was my favorite glass bowl," Jade retorted. "Because you are so vertically challenged, you ruined it."

"Are you calling me clumsy?"

My eyes landed on Stacey, Weston, and Hayley. Stacey and Weston were deep in conversation, probably discussing about Warren's well being. Hayley stared down at her porcelain plate, playing with her food.

"Danny," Abigail whispered so only I could hear. "I'm sorry about what happened."

"You didn't do anything, Abs," I said, smiling at her. "It's fine. If he's happy, then I'm happy for him."

"Weston obviously doesn't see what a great girl he was blessed with," Abigail said angrily. "He doesn't deserve you at all."

"Abigail, I wanted the break up. Not him. So he's not at fault."

"Still! He doesn't need to be gallivanting with other girls when he found his mate, does he?"

I stayed quiet for several seconds before voicing the question that has been on my mind. "Does she know about us?"

Abigail shook her head. "I think its better that way," she whispered. She looked over my head, her eyes widening slightly. "Oh, no."

I looked back to see Hayley coming towards us. She sat in Jade's chair – which was next to me – with a friendly smile on her face. "Hi guys," she said.

'Stop it,' I told my growling wolf. 'Being jealous won't solve anything.'

"Hi Hayley," Abigail said stiffly, plastering a fake smile on her face. She was interrupted when a crumpled napkin hit her cheek. Her smile fell and she turned to glare at Eli's smug face. "You're such an attention seeker, drama queen!"

Jet and Beau groaned as the couple argued again.

"Hey Hayley," I said, turning back to Hayley with the friendliest expression I could muster. I probably looked like a hyperactive chipmunk, but it was better than being stoic.

"Danny," she returned. "It's nice to finally meet you. Your group of friends had many good things to say about you. I was excited to meet you from the way they described you."

"Good things, I hope," I laughed awkwardly.

Although Hayley was being immensely nice and kind, I couldn't help but feel awkward around her. She was dating the man that was made for me – my soul mate. She loved my first love, my current love, and the person I will love forever no matter the circumstances.

"From the way your friends talked about you, I don't think there was anything bad to say," she laughed.

"Good, because I would have smacked them all," I joked.

We noticed Weston staring at the both of us. Hayley smiled at him and I averted my gaze elsewhere. It made me wonder if she knew about me and Weston's past.

"So," I cleared my throat. "You and Weston, huh?"

"Yeah," she gushed like a girly teenager. "We've been together for six months."

Even if I prepared myself for her answer, it still caused my stomach to twist into an agonizing knot. My wolf howled at the thought of her mate being with someone else. I ignored the growing ache in my chest and quickly shook off the feelings before Hayley saw.

"That's great," I said brightly although I wasn't feeling so bright at the moment.

"He's the best," she continued to gush. "I'm so lucky that he's my boy friend. He's really sweet, funny, and gosh, is he handsome."

"I'm happy for you two!" I exclaimed. My statement was half-true. I was happy that Weston was happy. "How did you guys meet?"

"As cliché as it sounds, I was walking to the store when I bumped into him. From there, our journey started." I resisted the urge to roll my eyes at her. She was one heck of a vulnerable, hopeless romantic.

I didn't know what to say next, because of my raging jealousy. I wasn't going to lie and say I wasn't jealous. I also wasn't going to lie and say Holly wasn't a friendly girl just because I envied her relationship with my soul mate. The hard truth was Weston had found a girl worth keeping.

"The dessert is finally ready," Jade sang, saving me from responding to Hayley. "Sorry it took so long. Jarred here was no help at all."

"I did mostly everything," he cried, following behind her. He held a huge cake in his hands and I resisted the urge to attack it. They knew how much I loved carrot cake and there it was, glorious on the porcelain platter. "I iced it, I piped out the letter, and I even baked it! Sorry dear, but you are one horrible cook."

"Anyways," Jade digressed, straying away from her embarrassment. "We made Danny's favorite cake to welcome Danny and Beau."

"You guys are too kind," I said, shooting appreciative smiles towards Jade and Jarred. I looked at everyone – including Weston – in the eyes with gratitude. "Thank you for welcoming me back and being friendly towards my cousin although he is a little slow – "

"Hey," Beau warned.

"I've missed you guys a ton and I'm glad that I'm here right now. You people have been amazing friends. Actually, you guys are like my family and you will always be my family," I said honestly while everyone at the table awed.

"The world must be ending," Jarred said, blinking. "I've never seen Danny be so nice."

"I agree," Eli and Jet said in unison.

"We've missed you," Stacey said, pushing her platinum blonde hair out of her face to give me a warm smile. "Welcome to Huntstown, Beau."

"Thank you," Beau said, smiling. "Thank you for taking me in."

"Oh, we'll take you in anytime, handsome," Jade said bluntly.

"I agree," Abigail giggled.

I laughed when Beau blushed and shot me a frightened look when Jarred and Eli growled. "Oh, relax," Abigail and Jade said simultaneously, laughing, and giving each other a high five.

"Welcome back, Danny," Everyone said while Stacey, Abigail, and Jade hugged me.

"The fabulous four are reunited," Jade cried.

"This is way to sentimental for my taste," I joked bitterly.

"Whatever," Stacey said. "I know you missed us."

"You love us," Abigail joined in.

"Hey," I yelled when I saw that Jarred already started eating the carrot cake. He froze with cream cheese on the corner of his mouth, brown eyes widening in horror. "You didn't just touch that carrot cake first!"

"Oh, I did," Jarred said smugly, taking another bite of the angelic cake on his plate.

I poked his belly. "You better watch out. You got big," I lied. Everyone roared in laughter.

"Oh please," Jarred said, not bothered by what I just said. He flexed his arm. "The only thing that got big were these muscles."

Everyone started teasing Jarred and the laughter and conversation just grew from there. It was loud, everyone fighting and joking with each other. I looked at my friends with a big, genuine smile on my face.

Although it was loud and crazy, I was happy to be back home.

***

My heart raced in my chest as the phone rang. Please be okay. The knots in my stomach constricted as I tightened my grip on my cell phone. Shaking slightly, I drew in an unstable breath.

I looked up at the dark sky, which was dotted with twinkling stars. There was a slight breeze, causing a rustle to come from the millions of leaves in the forest behind the pack house. It was silent as I sat on the porch steps, waiting for Darren to pick up.

"Hello," a tired voice answered from the other end.

"Dar," my voice shook. "What happened? How come you didn't call me? Did something happen with mom?"

"I'm sorry, Danny," He said. "I just didn't want to bother you. I knew the packs planned a welcome back dinner."

"Mom is my priority. It was the reason I came here."

"She's fine," Darren reassured with a lighter voice. "The doc said she'd be able to eat right in a couple of days."

"Can I visit?" I said, anxious to hold my mother in my arms.

"Sure, you can come over now, but she's sleeping," Darren said.

"Oh," I said slightly disappointed. "I think I'll just come over tomorrow after the meeting. She's resting. I don't want to bother her. She needs her rest."

"Okay, then I'm going over there to come see you," Darren said. I heard the jingling of keys. He yawned. "I'm so sorry that I wasn't there to welcome you home."

"Dar, just get some sleep. I'll come tomorrow. Don't worry. I would rather you take care of mom than welcome me home."

"Are you sure?"

"Of course," I smiled even if he couldn't see me. "Just so you know, I'm smiling right now.

"That's right, kiddo," I heard Darren's voice lace with happiness. "Hold your head up high and smile. Stand –"

"Stand up tall and remain strong. You are strong," I recited, remembering the words my older brother always told me when we were going through rough times. "You too, Dar," I sighed, hoping that my brother was okay. "Are you okay?"

There was a short pause before he sighed. "I'll be fine. Now go sleep. You must be tired from your road trip."

"See you tomorrow. Good night, brother. I love you."

"Love you too, little sis," Darren said, before the line went dead.

Tears slipped down my cheeks, wanting to embrace my family in my arms. I felt useless sitting here, crying while I could be over there to help Darren take care of my family. There was only one reason that made me take residency in the pack house for my stay in Huntstown.

I had a feeling that the only reason they were attacked was because of me and I didn't need to lead any more danger towards my injured mother.

"Are you okay?" I heard a familiar voice say. I closed my eyes, my chest clenching at the soothing, male voice. Although I hated that he had to see me like this, a shiver went down my spine.

I got up from my seat on the porch steps and turned to face Weston. His crystal blue eyes still held a lot of emotion. He slightly flinched when a traitor tear rolled down my cheek.

"I'm fine," I said distantly, walking around him to go back into the house.

"Ells," he whispered. The pain in my chest grew, hearing him use the nickname he gave me. I closed my eyes once again, walking towards the door as if I've never heard him.

"Ells," he said with concern. I froze when I felt his hand on my arm, causing the familiar warmth and tingles to spread all throughout my body. My wolf howled, wanting to be closer to her mate.

I refused to turn around to face him, feeling the tears roll down my cheeks some more. There were a lot of emotions surfacing now that I just talked to my brother and Weston finally wanted to talk to me after fourteen months.

"Yes?" I whispered, my voice quavered and I cursed myself for being so weak.

"Can we talk?" He asked after a short silence. He dropped his hand. I felt his eyes burning holes in my back.

"What do you want to talk about?"

"We need to talk – or I think we should talk – about the – about where we -," Weston sighed. "Can we talk about us?"

"There's nothing to talk about," I shrugged. Even if my back was facing him, I felt him flinch.

"We need to talk about us and I know you're probably wondering about Hayley," Weston said, his voice trembling.

"Wes, there's nothing to talk about, okay? It's my fault that we're not together anymore. I'm happy for you and Hayley. You deserve to be happy."

I didn't give him time to answer as I opened the back door and entered the house. Once again, I walked away from Weston with tears in my eyes.

Chapter 4

"First off, please welcome back Danny," Weston said to the crowd of people in front of him, motioning a hand towards me. "Also, please welcome her cousin Beau Wrode."

The crowd clapped with bright smiles on each of their faces. It was rare to see a pack meeting with this much people. It must be because the Crescent and the Stone pack decided to have today's meeting together.

It was also rare to see that the two packs got along well. They sat together, making small conversation. The men shook each other's hands while the women hugged each other.

All one hundred and seventy of us were cramped up in the meeting room in the Pack House. Everyone shared chairs, kids sat in their parent's laps, the men stood to the side of the room. The representatives of the pack – such as Jarred, Weston, Eli, Jet, Jade, Abigail, Stacey, Charles, Dustin, Alex,

Beau, and I – stood at the front. The only people missing were Darren and my mother.

The thought caused an ache in my chest, but I quickly shook it off. I couldn't wait to see them after the meeting. It wouldn't surprise me if I bolted out of the room before anyone else did once the meeting was adjourned.

"As you all know, I'm Alpha Weston Marshall of the Crescent Pack," my mate said, smiling a warm smile towards the werewolves. My wolf soared with pride at the mention of her mate's high title. He patted Eli's back. "This is Beta Elliot Cooper."

"I'm Alpha Jarred Hunter of the Stone Pack," my best friend said and flashed a perfect smile. He motioned towards Charles. "This is Beta Charles Porter."

Charles, Alex, and Dustin welcomed me home this morning. Although they didn't really spend much time around the Crescent pack because they couldn't really stand it, they were still great friends of mine.

I shot a warning look at Eli who looked like he was going to tear Charles into shreds. Charles rolled his eyes, still standing next to Abigail. "You better stay the fuck away from her, pup," Eli whispered only so we could hear. Alex and Dustin growled at Eli, protecting their Beta as an instinct.

"Look, Cooper, Abigail and I are just friends," Charles snapped. "I respect her decision to be with her soul mate. You have her now, so I don't know why you're getting your panties in a twist."

To refresh your memories, Charles and Abigail were in a relationship and were still in a relationship fourteen months ago. A month after I left, Abigail broke up with Charles, telling her she felt that it was wrong to date somebody else when she was blessed enough to have found her mate.

Charles let her go. Two months after that, Eli and Abigail started their relationship.

The Alphas shot a warning look towards their Betas, obviously telling them through the mind link that they needed to quit being immature.

After I left, I put a block up to hide what I was feeling and all my thoughts from Westin and the Crescent Pack. They didn't need to hear my true feelings or my exact reason for leaving.

"It's good to see all of you here," Jarred continued. "We are extremely proud to be the Alphas of such a dedicated pack. I'm pretty sure you are aware of why we called a meeting." There were a few slow nods, a blanket of fear and concern covering the people in front of us. "So, Alpha Weston will explain further."

Weston cleared his throat, before saying, "A few days ago, we were attacked by hunters in the forest with weapons laced with wolfs bane. From our discovery, they were customized guns, spears, and arrows to take down werewolves."

There were a few gasps, including my own. The pit of my stomach began to hurt from all the tension and the fear that started to build.

"No worries, there are no signs of hunters so far. They do not know where we live or where we walk. They just caught us while we were taking the special training that the representatives receive.

"Luckily, nobody was killed in this attack. We managed to take down the hunters. However, two people were severely injured. Please give a round of applause for the bravery of Jarred Hunter who took a knife for his mate, Jade Marshall," Weston said with gratitude. I clapped with the crowd, proud that Jarred had done that to protect Jade. "And to Ella Wrode, who unfortunately couldn't make it today because of her condition. She took the bullet for her son, Darren Saunders. We are completely lucky to have not lost such a brave woman."

I felt the tears build up in my eyes, but I didn't dare let it fall. I smiled with the relief that my mother had made it and clapped proudly with the crowd.

"Are you okay?" Beau said through the mind link. With Healers, it was impossible to block out each other. Healers were supposed to work together and it was forbidden to deny each other.

"Yes, cous. I'm just happy that my mom is okay."

"She's a Wrode!" Beau said, causing me to smile even bigger. "That's my Aunt Ella!"

"However, we are still in danger," Weston continued, bluntly. It was an Alpha's duty not to lie to their pack. "We got a lead on Rogues helping these hunters take down both our packs. It is true. Rogues and hunters have teamed up."

My mouth dropped open and there were loud gasps. The whole room started talking hysterically. Before it could get any crazier, Jarred and Weston said, "Quiet down!"

The whole room fell silent in a second. Beau and I were shocked, having to hear this for the first time. The other representatives kept a straight face, but I could tell they were as scared as everyone in this room was.

"Why?" I blurted out before thinking twice, causing everyone to look at us. I was genuinely curious. I held my head high, looking Weston square in the eyes. "What are their intentions?"

It took a couple of seconds for Weston to answer. He looked me straight in the eyes and then back at everyone in front of him. "We have something that the Hunters are after, but never in a million years will I give it to them."

In a second, the room was in complete chaos.

"What?" A guy with graying hair yelled.

"This is just ridiculous," a woman cried, clutching her three-year-old son to her.

"You would put your packs in danger because you refuse to give something up?" Another woman yelled.

"Enough," Jarred's voice roared through out the crowd. It shook the windows, causing a silence to fall upon the room. Everyone looked down, ashamed and scared. I, too, shrunk back a bit from the authority in his voice. "It is too valuable to be given up."

"What could it possibly be?" Beau said beside me, shock written across his features.

"I'm afraid that is confidential," Weston replied. "This meeting is adjourned. Please leave without drawing attention towards our pack house."

In an hour and a half, the conference room was emptied out and everyone had left. Alex, Charles, and Dustin had left. We all slumped down in the couches in the living area, deep in thought.

"What do the hunters want?" I brought myself to ask my friends.

"I have no idea," Jet replied. "Only the Alphas know."

At that moment, Jarred and Weston came out of the conference room. They looked exhausted and stressed. Jade shot up from her seat, hugging Jarred to calm him down. Weston walked towards the hallway that led to the front door. He was probably going for a run to let off some steam.

"Beau, are you ready to go?" I asked, getting up from my seat. I really wanted to see my family.

Beau nodded, following me to the front door. "That was intense," Beau said.

"Tell me about it."

"Are you ready to see your mom?"

"I can't wait to see her. I missed her so much."

"I can't wait to hear her compliments. I know what she's going to say already. She's going to thank me for being the doting cousin and she's going to say I'm immensely handsome," Beau joked. I elbowed him in the ribs and laughed.

"You better watch out. Once she found out what you said, she won't be complimenting you anymore," I said.

"I'm kidding," Beau said, throwing his arm around my shoulder. "I miss Aunt Ella and I really want to see her after the – uh – "

"The attack," I said bluntly. "Just say it, Beau. Avoiding it wouldn't change the truth."

"I'm sor – "

He went silent when we saw the scene in front of us. I froze, feeling the familiar ache in my chest. Only this time, it was ten times worst.

I've always felt it when he kissed another girl or the one time he made love to another girl. It was different when you saw it. It confirmed that whatever you were feeling was true.

Weston's back was faced towards us and Hayley was on the other side of the door. She smiled, before reaching up on her tiptoes to peck Weston on his lips. Although it was only a millisecond, my heart shattered and it felt like a cobra wrapped itself around my chest. I bit my lip, refusing to let the growl that threatened to escape. My wolf was angry.

Beau looked angry as he pulled me closer to his chest and pushed towards the door. "Excuse me," He said, rudely shoving passed Weston.

He put me in the passenger seat of my Land Rover and he climbed into the driver's seat. He drove out of there as fast as possible. However, I didn't miss the hurt look that crossed Weston's features when he looked at me.

After a couple of Beau's concerned glances, I said, "I'm fine, Beau."

"I don't believe you! You're so honest with everything else except yourself!"

I flinched, looking at him. I could tell he was angry by the way he clutched the steering wheel tightly, causing his knuckles to turn white. "He's an asshole," He continued.

"Forget it, Beau," I said, trying to change the subject.

"No, Danny! Why are you trying to run away from your problems with Weston?" He cried stubbornly.

"I'm not running away, Beau," I snapped. "If I were running away, I wouldn't have come here in the first place which brings me back to why we came here in the first place! I came here for my mom, not Weston!"

We arrived at my house in no time, the mini mansion looming over us. Beau and I sat there for a couple of second. Looking at me, he said, "You're right. I'm sorry."

"Beau, you're just being a good cousin," I smiled. "So thank you for looking after me."

"Always, Danny," Beau said. "Now let's get inside so Aunt Ella could compliment me."

I rolled my eyes, getting out of the car. Before I could open the door, it slammed open. Brown eyes stared at me, his brown hair swaying in the harsh winds. His smile graced his handsome face, before he engulfed me in his muscular arms.

"Darren," I screamed, hugging him tighter. I felt a few tears of happiness escape. "I've missed you so much."

"Little sister," He said, pulling back from me to look at me. "You've got some toned arms. Did this guy," Darren stopped to slap Beau's head. "work you too hard?"

"She was a weakling," Beau said, putting Darren in a headlock once Darren let go of me. "She couldn't even life a hollow block."

"Hey," I snapped. "Stop exaggerating!"

"Boys," a feminine voice laughed. "They think all girls are weaklings."

"Kelly," I shrieked, almost tackling the petite blonde-haired woman to the ground.

Kelly and I had definitely gotten closer when Darren and her came to visit me six months ago. We went shopping, sharing similar thoughts and our sarcasm towards Darren. She was like my older sister – which she was. To be precise, she was my older sister in law. Yes, she was human and yes, she was mates with my older brother.

"Danny, you're going to kill me," she choked.

I let go of her slightly, before saying, "Right. You're human."

"Did Beau teach you to be so cocky?" Kelly gasped, casting a teasing glare at Beau.

"Why does everybody blame me?" Beau cried.

"Because you're an idiot," all three of us said in unison, obviously used to saying this one statement to him.

"You guys are all mean," Beau said, crossing his arms over his chest like a five year old.

"Anyways, Kelly is making food since Aunt Fel is on a trip around the world," Darren said. "I'll take you to see mom."

My heart was pounding hard with every step we took towards her room. I flinched when I heard a strangled cough. Darren threw an arm around my shoulder, trying to comfort me.

The tears spilled out all at once when Darren opened the door, causing my heart to break. My mother lay in her bed, looking at us tiredly. Every blink was longer than it was supposed to be. Her translucent skin had sheen of sweat although the room was cold. Her dry lips turned up in a smile as she looked at us.

"Danny, my baby," she said hoarsely. "Why are you crying? Come here and give me a hug."

I came over to her, hugging her softly. Her arms shook as she lifted them slowly to go around neck. "Mom, I'm just so happy to see you."

Luckily, there were no wounds on her face because that would have hurt me even more. I did not dare remove the blanket around her. Because if I did, I would have seen the gauze wrapped around the area she was shot.

"I missed you, my baby," my mom said, smiling.

"Hey Auntie," Beau said happily, coming to give my mom a quick peck on the cheek.

"Oh, Beau, you're so handsome," my mom said, patting his cheek. "Thanks for taking care of Danny."

I rolled my eyes as Beau flashed me a knowing smirk. "You're welcome. Anything for my family."

"Did you find yourself a mate yet?" My mom asked, knowing of Beau's conquest to find his mate.

"No," Beau said darkly, before joking around. "I don't think anybody could handle this much strength and hotness."

"Better watch it, boy," my mom laughed tiredly. "Even if I'm weak, I could take you down."

"Why don't we let Danny and my mom have a little alone time right now?" Darren said, smiling at the two of us.

"So, how are you?" I asked when the it was just my mom and I.

"I'm fine, Danny."

"Mom," I said, fresh tears welling up in my eyes. "I'm sorry it wasn't there. I feel like it's my fault that you guys got attacked. I'm so sorry. You almost died because of me. I'm the reason for all this – "

"Nonsense, Danny," my mom scolded. "Stop blaming yourself for things that you had no intentions doing."

"It's the truth."

"Give me proof that it is then." When I stayed quiet, my mom continued. "Danny, you always blame yourself. You always tire yourself. None of this is your fault. Stop it. I got shot because I was protecting my children and I would rather die than let my children die."

"I love you, mom," I cried, laying next to her in her queen sized bed.

"Stop crying," My mom said. "How about you? Are you okay?

"I'm fine," I said, clueless. Why would she ask that question when I was clearly healthy and unwounded?

"I heard about Weston, honey," my mom whispered.

My heart constricted and my tears started falling even harder. Here, with my mom, it was hard to pretend I was okay with it. She would read the lie.

"I don't even know," I blurted before I could stop myself. "I was the one who broke up with him, but I didn't break up with him because I didn't love him anymore! I broke up with him because I didn't want him to get tangled up with my own problems for being a Healer. It hurts me to know he loves another girl. It hurts me to know that he's happy without me. It hurts me to know he's kissing and hugging somebody else. I'm pretending that I'm fine, but I'm far from it."

It was quiet for a moment, before my mother said, "Oh, honey, I'm so sorry. Just remember one thing."

"What is it?"

"Love is always going to find ways to kill people. That's the test. It's the test to see that two people will still love each other despite their challenges."

Chapter 5

While everybody was doing something productive and fun, I sat outside on the porch steps. I'm not usually one to wallow in self pity, but here I was being a Debby Downer. It angered me that I was being so weak and vulnerable, doubting everything in life and being such a pessimist.

Although my resistance to talk about Weston, it did help beneficially. It made me open my eyes to the fact that I wasn't completely at fault for my heart break at this moment. It took my mother to realize what everybody had been telling me, he didn't have to get into a relationship just because I wanted a little break. We were soul mates for crying aloud!

I missed him.

I missed his warm hugs. I missed our passionate kisses. I missed his teasing and his joking. I missed snuggling up next to him. I missed the sparks that flew whenever we touched. I missed his laugh. I missed his arrogant smirk. I missed everything about him.

What happened to us?

That's right.

I ended it.

My hands itched to run through his jet-black hair, which he still wore short. I wanted to stare into his blue eyes forever, knowing that nobody else in the entire universe would feel the way I did when I stared into them. I wanted to kiss his soft lips, anticipating the tingles that would erupt throughout my body in the next few milliseconds. He was an addiction, like my own drug – like my own coffee flavor and you all know how much I love coffee.

Ugh, I am such a hopeless romantic!

'You just lobe him,' my wolf teased me.

'You have got to be kidding me. You have to use that right now? Seriously? Thanks for bringing me down memory lane,' I snapped, remembering the first time that Weston told me he loved me. Although it should have pained me, I couldn't help the silly smile that crept its way onto my face.

'He still loves you too,' she whispered. My heart thudded against my chest before I laughed at her. 'You don't believe me?'

'He has a girl friend and to think I was the hopeless romantic. You're even worse.'

'GROWL!'

'You're so girly. Couldn't you just growl instead of actually saying it? That's like saying OMG instead of saying 'oh my gosh'.'

'I'm telling you, he still loves you.'

'Right, that would be the day Paula Dean stops clogging her arteries with butter.'

'You're such a pessimist.'

'And you're a nosy gossip girl.'

'Bitch.'

'You're the one that's a female dog … literally.'

'Can you just make up with him? I miss my big dog.'

'Ew, that's what you call Weston's wolf?' I scrunched up my nose, before I sighed sadly. 'I miss him too. I swear, it's like I could smell him right now.'

His manly scent wafted up my nose, causing my wolf to purr in delight. I inhaled, drinking it up. My eyes rolled back in contentment and I moaned softly.

"That's my favorite sound of all time," an amused voice joked.

I jumped a foot in the air, snapping my eyes to meet amused clear ones. He ran his hand in his dark hair giving me one of his genuine smiles. He sat next to me, looking at the dark forest in front of us.

I would have been angry that he approached, but there was just something about the way he approached me tonight that said he wasn't looking for a fight. For the first time in fourteen months, I agreed with him. I was tired of all this hullabaloo.

Yes, I just used hullabaloo.

"You're still as cocky as ever," I said, smiling slightly at the memories.

Weston smirked, causing my toes to curl. As cliché as it sounded, there was no other man that could measure up to to his looks. He was excessively handsome to compare.

"I see that you're still a cranky, old woman trapped in a teenage body," Weston joked.

I sighed inwardly. He was still the same. He didn't change much after all.

"You're comebacks are still lame. Come on, Marshall. Haven't I taught you anything?"

"It's hard for a student to learn if he had a crappy teacher."

"Touché," I smirked. "I thought you were hanging out with Eli."

"Eli decided to cut up Jade's undergarments," He said, chuckling. Oh gosh, that sound. It was music to my ears. "I didn't want to be there when Jade throws a tantrum."

In that precise moment, I laughed at perfect timing. There was a loud crash inside the house. "Elliot Cooper," Jade growled. "You are such an immature brat!" A high-pitched scream followed – a scream that only belonged to Elliot Cooper.

Weston and I erupted into laughter. Sure, it wasn't a laugh that made me hiccup, but I still appreciated the fact that I actually laughed in his presence. The silence that followed was actually comforting.

I couldn't believe that we were actually having a civil conversation.

"So, how's your mom?" Weston asked, genuinely concerned. I didn't know what possessed me, but there was just something about him that made me trust him.

"She's fine," I sighed. "I just wished I was there to save her. She wouldn't be suffering right now."

"It's not your fault," he said. Call me crazy, but I think he scooted the tiniest bit closer to me. "You didn't know it was going to happen. You should stop blaming yourself for everything, Ells."

"So, you and Hayley?" I asked. Well, in actuality, I blurted it out. I couldn't help it. The burning curiosity couldn't be contained any longer. In addition, I wanted to stop talking about my mom before I ended up having a break down again.

His eyes widened, before he scratched the back of his neck. "It's nothing," he said simply, shrugging.

For some reason, his answer angered me. I pushed my brown hair out of my face, sure that my green eyes were blazing with anger. "It's nothing?" I snapped. "What do you mean it's nothing?"

Was he using her? She was such a sweet girl. For him to be doing that to her was totally wrong. She did nothing wrong to him and he was kissing her up for a heartbreak.

"You wouldn't understand, Ells," Weston whispered, irritation blazed in his blue eyes.

"Oh, please enlighten me," I snapped sarcastically.

"It's better left unsaid, Danny."

"She loves you, you know," my voice started rising now. I stood up, facing him. "And you had to go and break her heart!"

In that moment, tears started spilling out of my eyes. I rubbed furiously at them. In that moment, I was trying to convince myself if I was talking about Hayley or me.

"What exactly are you trying to do?" I yelled.

"Danny," Weston said desperately. "I'm telling you. Ignorance is bliss."

"I'm in no mood for secrets right now."

"Why do you care, huh?" Weston said, his voice rising too. He was so close that I could feel the electricity buzzing around us. I looked up into his darkened eyes. "Why do you care what goes on between Hayley and me?"

"Stop trying to turn the tables, Weston," I sneered, poking him in the chest.

"Why do you care, Danny?"

"I asked you a question!"

"Why do you care?" Weston growled. "It shouldn't matter so much to you, Danny! You're the one who broke it off! So why the hell should you care?"

"Did it ever occur to you that I'm still in love you?" I snapped, tears rolling down my flushed face. I shoved him in the chest and punched him from the built in anger. "Just because I broke up with you doesn't mean you have to have a girl friend! You want to know why I broke up with you? I didn't break up with you because I didn't love you! I just didn't want you to get hurt and tangled up into my mess! You want to know why? Because I loved you too damn much to watch you get hurt!"

I drew in a shaky breath, sobbing loudly. I didn't know if Weston could understand me anymore with the way I was speaking. He didn't say anything, his eyes widening and staring down at me in shock.

"Stupid I, thinking that my own soul mate still loved me. Then there it was! The searing pain that almost made me die, Weston! I almost died because you made love to another woman! Does this mark mean nothing to you?" I asked, shoving my brown hair back and showing him the crescent shaped birthmark on my neck. "So, the answer to your question is pretty clear. I care because I'm still irrevocably in love with you."

He stayed quiet for a bit before his lips trembled. "I'm sorry," he whispered.

"You're not sorry," I snapped once again. My anger surfaced once again. "If you were sorry or if I meant anything to you, you wouldn't have been with Hayley!"

"Ells," Weston replied, broken.

"Don't, Weston," I held up my hand. "Don't pretend to care when you obviously don't. You're still that playboy and I was one of those stupid sluts who fell in love with his player ways."

"God damn it," Weston growled, his eyes turning black. He punched the cement wall of the house, leaving a dent on it. I automatically flinched back, although I knew he wouldn't hurt me. If you still loved me, you would have faith in our relationship! If you still loved me, you would have made sure that you would keep our relationship alive despite the drama that comes with being a Healer. If you still wanted a relationship, we would still fucking have one! Don't give me that shit that I didn't care for you when you gave the impression that you didn't love me anymore when we broke up! So stop being jealous of my relationship with Hayley!"

"You're an asshole," I screamed, shoving him in the chest.

"What the hell is going on here?" Jarred shouted, running out the back door. He put himself in the middle of Weston and I. Weston's eyes were no longer a crystal blue, but pitch black. His growls filled the silence in the air. Jet, Eli, Abigail, Stacey, and Jade were watching with wide eyes from the porch. Beau stood at my side, glaring at Weston.

"Step away, Hunter," Weston said, breathing in and out. "This is a conversation between me and Danny."

"This conversation has ended," Jarred said. "You need to calm the fuck down."

"Whatever," Weston muttered, looking at me before he ran off. His clothes shredded, his beautiful gray wolf sprinting into the forest.

"Beau, calm Danny down." It was only then that I realized my fur was itching to escape my skin and my growls escaped low and vicious. "There might be hunters in the forest and the last thing we need is a dead Alpha," Jarred ordered.

My blood ran cold, stopping my growls and snapping me out of my anger. I watched as Jarred ran off towards the woods in his wolf form. After hearing what Jarred said, I wanted to follow him to make sure that my mate was okay.

"Danny, you're not going there," Beau ordered, reading my thoughts through the mind link. He was a higher Healer than I was, so I was possessed to stay where I was.

I looked at him angrily, storming into the house with fresh tears running down my face. I ignored the calls of my friends and cursed myself for being so stupid.

'Please be okay,' my wolf whispered at the same time I did.

Chapter 6

Beau and I decided to do some investigation on our own after the reminder last night that the hunters and the rogues were still after us. After all, we were Wrodes and Wrodes do not like to just stand around and wait for something to happen. Beau and I were taking actions into our own hands.

"That asshole was lucky that there were no hunters or rogues in the woods last night," Beau said, sitting comfortably in the passenger seat.

"Tell me about it," I muttered, clutching the steering wheel. "I don't know what I would've done if he died."

Beau simply sighed, staying quiet. This whole morning, he's been overprotective of me, casting deadly glares at Weston. He complained more than I did about this whole situation. Everyone complained more than I did. Obviously, they weren't too happy with him at the moment.

When I found out he made it home safe, I cried tears of relief. I was worried sick and if he died, I would've hated myself for the rest of my life.

I pulled into the small parking lot of "The Big Shot". It one of the three stores that sold guns in Huntstown. We investigated one of the other two gun stores prior to approaching this place. However, it was shot down the minute we saw how rusty their guns were and how bad business was running in the place.

I looked at the small, rectangular shop with fear. Leave it to me to think of the worst-case scenarios every single time. I was scared that somehow these humans would find out what we were. It was risky walking into a place with guns. We could be dead any minute if they found out.

When Beau and I entered the shop, the small bell on the door rang signaling our arrival. My stomach clenched when my eyes saw the various guns sitting on the shelves and hanging on the walls. Beau – who always stayed calm – snorted at a picture of a man next to the bear he shot, smiling proudly. My eyes widened when it rested on spears identical to the ones I saw the night of the warehouse incident.

"Beau," I whispered, gripping his forearm. "Those are the ones the hunters used when my dad planned the attack on us."

His eyes widened slightly before he smirked. "Then I think we found the right place."

"How could you be so ca –"

"Hello," a raspy voice greeted. We turned around to face a skinny man dressed in faded jeans and a flannel shirt. His dark, curly hair was pushed under a blue, faded cap. He smiled, showing a set of yellowing teeth. According to his worn out tag, his name is Ron. "Do you need any assistance?"

"Yes," Beau said looking around the place with confusion. "I don't know much about guns, but we just moved in with our family. We're trying to get rid of dogs that we've sighted in our back yard. We have a little sister and we're concerned about her safety. What are your suggestions?"

I tried to hide the smile on my face. Beau was good at acting. I wouldn't be surprised if he made it into Hollywood with his charming good looks and his acting skills.

"Ah," Ron muttered, smiling wider like he knew something we didn't. "Dogs. That is a big problem here at Huntstown. Follow me."

We followed him towards a set of rifles hanging behind the register. He went behind the counter, taking a gun off the rack and handing it to Beau. Beau took it cautiously, examining the gun.

'Does this look familiar?' Beau asked through the mind linked, fingering the black metal.

'No. You would smell the wolfsbane. This is not what we're looking for. It's just a regular rifle.'

"So, why did your family decide to move to such a small town?" Ron asked curiously.

"Our father is a geologist. We move around a lot to small towns. We usually stay for two to three years and then we move again," Beau lied smoothly.

"How old are you, son?" Ron asked, scratching his wrinkled face. "Are you aware that we can't sell guns to minors and you must present a valid gun license when purchasing a gun?"

"I'm nineteen, sir," Beau smiled. He pulled out his wallet and showed his gun license to Ron. Beau didn't lie about that one thing. He actually possessed a gun license, but did not own any guns.

"So, tell me about these big dogs," Ron suggested, leaning over the counter.

Beau put down the gun and looked at him, "Well, I don't know what steroids Huntstown feeds them, but they're huge! This one I saw was the size of a bear and it growled constantly. We locked up the house, scared that it was going to attack us."

"It didn't leave for about an hour," I piped in for the first time. Ron looked at me with curious eyes. "We called the police, but they thought we were crazy."

"That's what the police always say," Ron finally said. "They don't believe a single thing about those huge dogs."

'Bingo,' Beau said excitedly through the mind link.

"You've seen these huge dogs too?" I whispered.

"Countless of times," Ron waved off. There was a mischievous look in his eyes. "Have you guys ever heard of werewolves?"

"What the hell is a werewolf?" Beau asked, looking at Ron weird. I almost laughed when Ron smirked.

"Come on, kids," Ron said smugly. "You guys have a lot to learn."

'This guy is so gullible. Any werewolf could walk into here and find his secret stash of wolfs bane,' Beau laughed through the mind link.

'He's smarter than you think. Once he finds out they're a wolf, he could just grab one of those guns from hell and shoot them dead in a couple of seconds.'

'Oh,' Beau realized, looking at me with fear.

We followed Ron, going through the door behind the counter. He led us through a long hallway and into a door that read 'Caution: Electricity panel. Enter at own risk.' Ron took out a key, opening the metal door.

"Um," Beau said simply, looking at the wires and panel box in the small room. "You wanted to show us the power room?"

"Watch, kid," Ron winked. He went to the far right of the small room and took out one panel from the wood wall. My eyes widened when a hidden white door appeared.

"Where are you taking us?" I asked, pretending to be scared. It was all part of the act.

"I want to show you kids the guns we use to take down those we – big dogs," Ron said excitedly. He opened the door, which had a small staircase that led to another door a level down. We followed him in the dimly lit passageway to a metal door. "You'll be amazed."

Ron opened the metal door and I cringed as the familiar smell hit me like a freight train. Each inhale burned holes in my lungs slowly. The amount of wolfs bane found in this room was enough to drain the energy from my body slowly.

Beau cringed when he smelt it, grabbing my arm in fear. 'Calm down, Beau,' I reassured him. 'You're going to make it obvious.'

Ron turned on the lights of the room, my stomach twisting when it landed on each deadly weapon piled up inside the room. I gasped lowly so only I could hear it. This definitely is hell on earth.

Ron inhaled deeply and said, "Personally, I love the smell of wolfs bane. What do you guys think?"

"It smells like flowers. I'm not really a flower person," Beau dismissed, beads of sweat forming on his forehead.

"What's wolfs bane?" I asked curiously, my eyebrows knitting together.

"It's a rare flower grown underground," Ron states as if it was his prized possession. "We boil it to mix its essence and herbs with the water. We soak the bullets and knives in them for a total of forty-eight hours so it is useful."

"I don't understand," Beau acted. "What's so special about wolfs bane?"

"Wolfs bane is a powerful medicine," Ron smirked. "We've been trying to get rid of those big dogs for years, but regular guns weren't working. We found out that once this medicine makes contact with those dogs, it is enough to sicken them and kill them."

My wolf growled, but I forced it down. I wanted to smack Ron for being so evil. After all, what did werewolves do to harm humans?

Beau and I look at the guns, but we refused to touch it.

"How much is your cheapest gun?" Beau asked. I looked at Beau with shock.

'Play along,' Beau linked.

"The AR-15 rifle is around nine hundred sixty-five dollars."

Beau whistled, running a hand through his light brown hair. "That's a lot for a gun."

"We charge a lot because of its wolfs bane."

"Could we possibly get a better price?" I asked Ron, giving him a pleading look. "We really need to get rid of those big dogs around our house for the safety of our baby sister and we don't have the money."

We were heading back up to the main store already and I was nothing but glad to get out of that hellhole. Ron was quiet for a moment before he walked us to the entrance. "Well, my boss will be here on Wednesday if you kids are willing to come back and buy it. I'm pretty sure he'd make a deal with you guys."

Beau nodded, looking over Ron's head at a big portrait on the wall. There were about fifty guys with guns and big smiles on their faces. "Do you guys have a mafia or something?" Beau joked, pointing towards the portrait.

Ron laughed and patted Beau's back. "That is my crew, son. We love hunting. It's our passion. Just the other day, we attacked those big dogs. We lost a few members of our crew, but that is our motivation to get back at those creatures. We have to do it for our fallen heroes."

I resisted the urge to roll my eyes. He talked about his crew as if they were the military, protecting the United States. At the same time, the hairs on my arm stood on end. Once again, we were faced with the reality that there were people who wanted to abolish us.

"Great," Beau plastered on a fake smile. "We would love to talk to your boss."

We left the store, driving away as quickly as possible. Beau slumped down in his seat giving me a tired look. "I can't believe we got a lead. All we have to do is meet the boss and see where to go from there."

"Yup," I said, popping the p.

"That's what you had to go through?" Beau whispered after a minute of silence. The tears threatened to spill any moment from the raw memories. I blinked it back, swallowed hard, and nodded. "I'm sorry you went through a lot."

I didn't know how to reply, so I nodded again. Beau sighed and decided to change the subject. "So anyways, Eli and Weston," he said on a lighter tone, spitting the name Weston out. "asked if we could show them the basic training that Healers undergo each week. So we're going to train the representatives' tomorrow morning."

Chapter 7

- -

NOT EDITED! ENJOY! (:

"Oh, come on, I don't want to hit a girl," Eli whined, stomping like a five year old. He crossed his arms over his bare chest, pouting his lips.

The representatives of the Crescent and Stone pack were giving Beau and me their undivided attentions. Although we were in September with the weather getting much colder, the men were shirtless and the women wore tank tops and sweats. Leave it to werewolves to sweat buckets with the temperature below sixty degrees Fahrenheit.

My mind was still reeling with the fact that we found a lead towards our investigation. This was beneficial. We would know how to better prepare ourselves when the hunters and the rogues decide to attack us. However, for now, Beau and I kept our investigation between us until we get farther into it.

"That's not the reason you want Beau instead of me, is it?" I teased, circling around Eli. "You obviously don't think I'm a challenge."

The first part of our training consisted with working out in our human forms, which most packs do. One thing we try to avoid is our animalistic side dominating our human side. That would lead to many tragedies and deaths.

As Healers, we start with grappling. I remember when I first started training with the Healers. I was pinned down in a second flat. By now, I was stronger and faster.

Therefore, here I was circling Eli while Beau and Jet already started grappling. Eli complained when he found out he was assigned to me. He thought I wasn't as challenging as Beau was.

"It's not that," Eli lied, eyes widening. "I don't want to hit a girl."

I used my inhuman speed to grab Eli's arm, pin him on the ground face down, and sit on top of him. Eli groaned when I pushed his arm farther behind his back. There were a few snickers from the people watching.

Weston's gaze made my skin tingle with heat. I tried to ignore it, but the lust in his eyes made me want to jump him right there and then. However, I had to remember that he wasn't mine and I wasn't his anymore.

"Just a little tip," I said loudly so everyone could hear. "Do not underestimate your opponents. Even if they are girls. Expect the unexpected."

"I wasn't ready," Eli defended, his words muffled by the ground. "Let's try this one more time."

I nodded, getting up to my feet and dusting the grass off my black tights. Eli lunged for me, but I dodged it. I yawned when I dodged another one of his lunges. I smirked.

"Show off," Eli muttered.

When Eli got a hold around my waist, I let him tackle me to the ground. He smiled, thinking he got me. However, I took a grab of his arm and twisted it. He let out a painful groan before laying in the grass next to me.

"You're good," Eli gasped, shaking out his arm. He ran in the direction of the lake.

When I looked at Beau, he moved on to Abigail telling her tips while she nodded. Jet had already started running towards the lake where he would have to swim ten laps and meet the rest of the group in the woods to play a game of hide and seek. Hide and seek was another way of testing your senses.

I remember the time that Weston helped me trained. That was one of my favorite training exercises. I quickly shook off the painful memories, smiling at Jade as she approached me.

Jade and I circled around each other, her blue eyes shining with anticipation. When we neared each other, she made a quick lunge to the left as a fake. This caught me off guard. I moved to the opposite side as an instinct like she had planned. She quickly caught my legs in her small arms, tackling me to the ground.

"You go, baby!" Jarred yelled.

"You're better than Eli," I laughed when I managed to pin her down. "Now, just keep that up and you'll do fine. Go run."

"Bossy," Jade smirked before saluting. "Yes, boss."

"Ready to be taken down?" Jarred asked, smirking smugly as he approached me.

"Don't be so cocky, pretty boy," I smirked back.

Jarred was actually better than you think. He circled around me in his inhuman speed about three times. This was enough to have me confused. When I moved to get him, he dodged me and quickly wrapped his arm around my waist before tackling me to the ground. With my face in the dirt, I tried to wriggle free from his tight hold on my arms.

"In your face, Danny," Jarred hollered, his laughter booming in the air.

When Jarred felt my body go slack, he loosened his hold on me. This gave me enough time to turn around and slip from underneath him. When I was free, I grabbed his leg and flipped him in the air. He landed with a groan before I put my foot on his back.

"Tip, never trust your enemies," I smiled, laughing at him.

"That was no fair!" Jarred cried, getting up with a scowl on his face.

"It was fair, J," I rolled my eyes.

When I looked up, Jarred had an amused smile on his face. He pointed at my right cheek, before bursting into laughter. "You have shit on your face!" Jarred screamed.

I felt the blood rush up to my cheeks before I wiped my face with my hand. "That is not poop! That's mud," I defended, looking at the mud on my face.

"Whatever you say ... shit face," Jarred smirked, running away before I could hit him.

I took my towel from the ground, wiping the mud off my face before turning to look at who was left. My body froze as Beau and I stared at an uncomfortable Weston.

"So," Weston said, looking between Beau and me.

'Go, Danny,' Beau linked. I could see the smug smirk on his face. 'I can't wait to take this dog down. I think he'd match a black eye.'

As much as I was angry towards Weston, I couldn't stand to see Beau beat him up in anger. I didn't want Weston to get hurt in all honesty. I was scared of what the outcome would result in after their brawl. Weston could kick us out anytime. Beau would kill him. Weston would beat Beau to a pulp if Beau angered him. Therefore, I did the unthinkable.

"Beau, why don't you start the training with the others," I suggested, smiling sweetly at my cousin. Weston eyes widened in shock.

'Danny, what are you doing?'

'Just do this ... for me. I'll be fine. I need to talk to Weston,' I lied.

'If he hurts you, then link me, okay? Then, I won't hesitate to kill this ass,' Beau said after a while of contemplating.

"If you hurt her," Beau growled. "I will kill you."

Weston simply rolled his eyes. "I'd like to see you try."

"Are you calling me out, pup?" Beau seethed, walking up to Weston. "You're lucky Danny cares too much for you to see you hurt. Considering, you hurt her practically almost every day."

I cringed at Beau's words. He didn't have to mention that. Weston growled when Beau walked away, before he lowered his eyes to look at me.

When Beau was out of sight, Weston stared at me with a look that I didn't even want to see right now. I felt like crying, the tears on brink of escaping. I held it in and stared right back.

Weston walked forward, close enough to grab my limp hand softly. I closed my eyes, feeling the tingles that shot all throughout my body from the small contact.

"Ells," Weston's strained voice broke through the tense silence. "I know you won't believe me, but I'm sorry. I'm sorry for putting you through this. I'm sorry for hurting you."

Suddenly, I felt angry. He wasn't sorry. If he were, he wouldn't even be doing what he did.

"You're not sorry," I growled, my wolf angry too. I grabbed his hand with inhuman speed and I pin him to the ground with more force than necessary.

I tried to ignore the heat that was around us from being so close. I tried to forget that he was shirtless and that my hands where pressed on his muscular back. I tried to smell the fresh soil and grass instead of his scent. I tried, but I was failing.

"I don't expect you to understand," Weston groaned when I dug my knee into his back. He stayed there for a while before turning us around with his Alpha strength and speed. He pins my arms above my hand, straddling my waist. "You need to calm down. You're grappling out of anger."

"And?" I growled, turning us around so that I was on top. I let go of his arms, so I could throw my hands in the air in sarcasm. "Is that a surprise?"

I pushed his face down with my hands, waiting for him to tap out. He didn't even budge. He looked at me with seriousness, before running his hands from my ankles to my hips agonizingly slow. "You need to calm down," he said.

I froze, relishing the heat of his hands on my legs. The only thing separating the skin-to-skin contact was the thin fabric of my leggings. It took me a couple of seconds to regain composure, remembering what was really going on here.

Now, I was furious. He was playing me again. He was doing all of this while he had a girl friend who loved him very much. Hayley didn't deserve the same heartbreak that I went through.

I growled at him, baring my canines. Weston's crystal blue eyes widened before he turned around without struggle. I placed my hands on his chest to push him off, but I froze. My growls came short when I felt his face near my neck.

I couldn't think anymore. I couldn't remember why I was angry. In fact, I think I forgot that I was angry when he placed his hands on my hips. Because my shirt rode up a little, his thumbs stroked circular patterns on the bare skin of my tummy.

I drew in a shaky breath when I felt his hot breath on my neck. My hands on his chest somehow found its way on to his shoulders. I gripped it when he ran his nose along my neck, inhaling deeply. "Calm down, please," Weston whispered, kissing his mark.

I shuddered, drinking in this moment that I have missed so much.

He pulled away, looking at me with his darkened eyes. His dark eyes melted into his blue ones as he stared at me with longing. I could feel my heart beat freeze as I saw him closer and closer. He stopped and just looked at me.

I couldn't take it any longer. I lifted my head off the ground, brushing my lips with his for a fraction of a second. With the low moan that escaped Weston's lips, I think I could die of cardiac arrest. The tingles and the heat intensified and I could hear my wolf purring. Dropping my head back to the ground, I tangled my hands into his black hair.

He looked at me, coming closer and closer until we were an inch apart.

"Weston? Jade? Is anyone there?" A familiar female voice called out. I could hear pounding on the door of the house.

"What was that?" I whispered, brushing my lips with his once again.

"I don't care," he said.

"Is anyone home?" The voice said again. Then my werewolf hearing picked up its muttering. "I swore Weston told me he'd take me on a date today."

The moment came crashing down like a bucket of ice-cold water. Weston didn't seem to notice, still looking at me. I frowned, feeling the tears escape. I'm such an idiot! I fell for him again!

"What's wrong?" Weston asked, dark eyebrows knitting together in confusion. He brought his hand up to wipe my tears, but I quickly pushed him off. I got up and started walking away from him. He stayed on the ground, trying to process what is happening. "What happened?"

"Um, Hayley is at the front door. Don't forget you have a date today," I turned around to face him. He flinched when he saw my flushed face, tears falling freely. In that moment, I didn't care. His face flashed with irritation. When he was about to say something, I stopped him. "Forget what happened, okay? It was a mistake."

I ran into the house and up the stairs, ignoring Weston's calls.

Chapter 8

"So, nothing went wrong with you and Weston?" Beau asked for the thousandth time. He sounded surprised, looking at me over his sunglasses with skepticism. "So how come the two of you disappeared after your grappling session?"

"Nothing," I lied smoothly, feeling guilty for hiding things from Beau. Hey, they do say that ignorance is bliss. "He had a date with Hayley and I called my mom."

I wasn't completely lying. Weston did have a date with Hayley and I did call my mom to vent out everything that happened. My mom just sighed, telling me that we wouldn't be able to fight this any longer.

That hard truth scared me.

"Right," Beau said with disbelief, leaning back in the passenger seat. "Whenever you're comfortable enough to stop lying to me, I'll be here."

I gulped, staring hard at the road in front of me. Good thing we decided to discuss this while I was driving. It gave me a distraction and he didn't have to see the guilt in my eyes.

"So, what do you think this boss guy is like?" I asked, digressing from the previous topic.

I didn't feel like talking about Weston today and I didn't feel like dealing with him. I was lucky that we didn't bump into each other in the kitchen as usual because I knew he wanted to talk about what happened yesterday. Weston was one to look for closure and to clear everything up.

I was one to run away. Beau was right after all.

"He's probably some bald headed man who wears Yankees caps and still lives with his mother," Beau said with disgust. "What vile humans. They attack those who didn't even do anything in the first place. Haven't they heard of animal abuse?"

"You do realize you called us animals, right?" I asked, raising my eyebrows.

"You know what I mean," Beau muttered. "I just can't wait to figure out this whole case, find out what to do, and bring down the people who hurt Aunt Ella."

"Revenge is not the answer."

"Aren't you angry at the people who hurt your mother?"

"Yeah, I am angry," I stated the obvious. "But I never see the point in revenge. All it does is prove who the biggest immature one is. I want to end this fight, not give them any other reason to get back at us."

After a couple of seconds, Beau said, "I guess you're right."

When we pulled up in the familiar parking space, I stared at the small red and white building. It's sign was worn out, peeling red paint. The glass windows and doors showed the interior of the store, empty guns lined up.

"Who the hell names their store 'The Big Shot'?" Beau scoffed. "Show offs."

"You're just biased because these people are trying to kill us," I laughed, slightly cringing at the thought. "Come on, drama queen. It's show time."

When we entered the small store, a skinny man with a faded blue cap looked up from his book on the counter. "Kids, I knew you'd show up," Ron called out in his raspy voice.

"Of course," Beau said, plastering a fake smile identical to the one on my face.

"How are you kids today?" Ron asked as if he knew us for a long time. "How are you liking Huntstown?"

"Huntstown is interesting," I said, examining a picture of Ron near a dead elk.

"Sure is!" Ron noticed me scrutinizing his photo. He smiled at me, obviously proud at his accomplishment. "That was two weeks ago. I shot it with my rifle. It was huge! It was the biggest dear Huntstown men have ever hunted. I was proud of myself for taking down that monster."

"Like I said, something must be in the water here. These animals are huge," Beau joked, before getting back to business. "So, is your boss here?"

"Yeah, he's just in the back. I'll get him for you," Ron said before disappearing into the back hallway. "Henry, the kids I was telling you about are here," we heard him say.

When Henry came out of the hallway, the first thing I noticed was the long scar across his cheek. No doubt was it from one of his hunter endeavors. His smile was big and friendly. You'd think he was one of those car sales person who tried to convince you to buy the most expensive car in the lot. His brown and white hair was cut short and tidy. When he smiled, the corners by his brown eyes crinkled. He had the hunters built.

"Hello, I'm Henry," He said, sticking his hand out.

"Beau," my cousin introduced with a smile, shaking his hand firmly.

"Danny," I simply said, giving his hand a timid shake.

"So, Ron here tells me that you're looking for a gun because you've spotted huge dogs around your house," Henry says, making it sound like a question.

"Yes, that is correct," Beau confirmed.

"Where do you live?" Henry asks casually.

When Beau doesn't answer, I pipe in. Beau doesn't know Huntstown like I do and I knew he would stumble upon that question. "In Bello Avenue, near the forest."

"Oh, yes, there has been sighting there," Henry says, still smiling. He turned back to Beau, patting a hand on his shoulder. "You look like a strong man, son."

My eyes widened, knowing exactly what he was going to ask Beau. It was written over his prideful face. Ron was literally jumping in excitement, smiling brightly.

'Shit,' Beau linked.

'Just keep calm, Beau. Refuse the offer like a normal person would.'

'Even if I were a normal person, I wouldn't join their group! They hardly know me!'

"I will sell the gun to you for five hundred, but on one condition," Henry continued. "We need a young man on the group who's strong and healthy. Since you've seen the special guns down in the basement, we figured you'd be a great addition. The Huntstown men would be honored if you decide to join us."

"As much as that sounds like a great offer," Beau says, pretending to think hard about the proposal. "I'm not daring enough to take on a responsibility like that. I have two sisters to take care of because my father is hardly around. I'm sorry."

Ron's face fell completely, looking like a lost puppy. Henry's smile dropped slightly, but he still smiled nonetheless. "You could take care of them by taking those dogs down," Henry reassures Beau, trying to convince him.

"Actually," I say, bringing the attention towards me. "We just came here to share our gratitude towards the brave men who protect the community. Ron told us about your massive attack a few days ago. We only noticed now that we haven't seen the dogs around."

Gag.

"I guess you scared them away," Beau smiles, patting Henry's shoulder this time. "So we thank you and we just dropped by to tell you that we don't need the gun anymore because we have brave men already. Thanks again for the offer."

After a couple of minutes of contemplating, Henry smiles. "We do what we can, right Ronnie?"

Ron nods his head hard, like he's afraid to disappoint his boss.

"If you ever change your mind," Henry persists, taking out a small white card from his pocket and writing something down on it. "Feel free to call me."

Beau takes the paper, stuffing it into his wallet. We mutter our goodbyes before shuffling out of the suffocating room. Piling into my Land Rover, we both sigh simultaneously.

"That was unexpected," Beau finally said. "I was afraid that if I decline their offer, they were going to figure out I was a werewolf. Thanks for saving me back there."

"Beau, don't be afraid," I told him although I was scared myself. "Everything will turn out alright."

"You don't know that." When I don't say anything, he adds, "What do we do now?"

"I don't know, cous," I whisper. "I don't know."

***

"Hey, best friend," I say, plopping down on the couch and ruffling Jarred's blonde hair.

Jarred lowers down the volume to his horror movie while I throw my feet over his lap. When he pushes them off, I bring it back up. "You're irritating," Jarred jokes, poking my side.

"You're just jealous that I'm cooler than you," I smirk, grabbing popcorn out of his bowl.

"Says the girl that was too scared to skip on Senior Skip Day."

"Hey, there's a difference between being a delinquent and being cool," I defended.

"So, what happened with you and Weston yesterday?" Jarred smirks. "Don't lie to me either. Your scent was so strong on Weston when we had our Alpha discussion."

"J," I rolled my eyes, trying to push down the blush that dared to color my cheeks. "We were grappling. Of course my scent would be on him."

"Yeah, that's what Weston said," Jarred waved off. "You grappled with me, Jade, and Eli. Your scent wasn't as strong as it was on him. He was also distracted, looking like a lovesick puppy."

"You're imagining things," I muttered, sure I was as red as a tomato now.

He was distracted?

"Ha! You're blushing!" Jarred yelled, pointing his finger at my face. "Spill."

"You're such a gossip girl."

"No, I just care for my best friend."

"Fine," I huffed. "Wealmostkissedandthingsweregettingprettyintense-butHayleycameinwhichisprettygood."

"What?" Jarred smirked, obviously catching what I said. "I didn't understand you."

I sighed. "We almost kissed and things were getting pretty intense. I blame myself. I initiated it. Hayley interrupted our almost kiss, so it was perfect timing."

"I knew it," Jarred smiled.

"Why are you smiling? Aren't you supposed to be angry or something?"

"No," Jarred said, shaking his head. "I have a mate and I'm kind of hoping you two will forgive each other like normal mates do."

"Whatever," I wave off, trying to change the subject. "Why are you by yourself?"

"Jade went somewhere," Jarred said, a frown replacing his smile.

"Where did she go?"

"She and Weston went to visit their dad at The Cell. The Experts permanently locked their dad's werewolf abilities and he's going to be locked up for life," Jarred said, clutching his hands into fist.

My eyes bulged out of their sockets while my mouth flew open. Their dad – previous Alpha – was in jail? My heart pounded, remembering what Weston told me about the man.

He used to abuse Jade because she reminded him too much of his deceased wife.

I knew how much Weston was hurt because of his dad's doings and it pained me to know I didn't know that his dad had went to jail. It pained me to know that something tragic must've happened that caused their dad to end up where he is now. Did he beat up Jade? Did Weston have to call the Experts on his own father?

Right when I was about to say something, I heard the front door open and close softly. Jarred got up to hug Jade who sobbed softly into his gray sweatshirt. Weston walked past the living room and out onto the porch with his head hung low.

Before I knew it, I found myself sitting next to him on the porch steps.

Chapter 9

N ot edited!

ENJOY!

It was a comfortable silence. The wind was a slight breeze, causing our hair to move around us. It took me a couple of minutes to talk. I was afraid to break the peacefulness that we actually had right now.

I knew it was a stupid question, but I asked anyways. "Are you okay?" I muttered, looking at his face.

As redundant as I sound, I couldn't get over how handsome Weston was. Even when he was angry or sad, he was still as handsome as ever with his defined jaw, strong cheekbones, and blue eyes framed by dark eyelashes that any girl would envy. His lips were set in a thin line.

"I'll be okay," he mumbled.

"I heard about your dad being locked up," I said. He nodded.

"Do you want to talk about it?" I stuffed my hands in my pocket, looking at his profile.

He hung his head down, before picking it up to stare at nothing in particular.

"I came home after a meeting with the representatives to grab some stuff Jade wanted. My dad was drunk as usual, slurring out and crying about how much he missed my mom. I decided to ignore it. I didn't know Jade was downstairs with him. She hasn't even been home since the last time he hit her. Remember when I told you about that story?" He looked at me when I nodded.

"She was telling him that my mom was in a better place and according to Jade, he nodded and said that Jade was right. He told her he was hungry, so Jade cooked him food.

"All of a sudden, I heard a huge crash and Jade screaming. I ran out as fast as I could. I saw my sister on the ground with the pan of hot food on her. She looked like a wreck. She was crying. Her hair was all over the place. She had a bruise on her cheek. For a werewolf to have a bruise, they must've been hit hard," Weston's voice quavered when he talked about how he discovered Jade. I scooted closer, putting a hand on his shoulder for comfort.

"You don't have to talk about it if you don't want to," I whispered. In all honesty, I was scared for him to go on. It felt like my ears were deceiving me. I wanted to cry for my mate – I felt the emotions he was feeling. I felt sick listening to what Jade had to go through.

"It's okay," Weston said. "So anyways, I saw my dad with the pan in his hand. It was raised, like he was about to hit her again. I jumped in front of Jade, pushing my dad back. He stumbled, looking at me angrily. If he wasn't locked up from his werewolf abilities, he would've shifted.

"He started yelling at me for protecting my sister – the girl that was a stupid idiot in his eyes. Imagine what Jade must've felt hearing that from her own dad. I asked him why he was doing this to his own daughter. He only laughed and said that Jade made food our mom always made. Well, of course Jade did. She learned how to cook from my mom.

"When I told him he was an asshole, I told him that was the last time he was ever going to see us. I started picking Jade off the floor, comforting her. The next thing I know, he took the kitchen knife and threatened us. I pushed Jade behind me, telling my dad to calm down. He was angry so he slashed my arm pretty deep," Weston sighed, picking up his shirtsleeve to point out a light scar on his muscled bicep. Now that he pointed it out, I was well aware of it. I gasped lowly, picking up a shaking hand to trace it with my index finger.

Looks like we had a lot in common. Both of our dad's harmed us.

Fate had a funny way of choosing mates for people.

"Soon after, an Expert and Jarred showed up in the kitchen. Jade later told me she linked Jarred for help. The Expert took down my dad and because they had powers that we don't, paralyzed him.

"So that's how my dad ended up being locked up. We visited him today because the Experts called us in for a meeting. Our dad was actually sober! What also was hard to believe was the repetitive apologies coming from him."

Weston sighed, breathing hard. He still didn't look at me. Before I could think twice, I wrapped my arms around his neck and hugged him. He was shocked, but he wrapped his arms around my waist.

"You and Jade didn't deserve that," I said genuinely, still holding on to him. "I'm sorry it happened."

"Thanks," he said when we let go.

"So what's going to happen to him?"

"He's going to be locked up for life. Werewolves are into family because they have this mentality that fate has given you a beautiful gift if you had a family. If you physically harm your loved ones with no valid reason, you committed a crime."

"How do you feel about your dad being locked up?"

"He deserves it, but I also think it's good for him. He'll get better."

"How often do you visit him?"

"Every month, we have a meeting with him. It's harder for Jade. He did say a lot of nasty things to her."

"Jade is a fantastic daughter. Your father was wrong," I defended, sticking my hands into my coat pocket.

"Thanks, Danny," Weston smiled, looking at me. "You're the only one I've actually talked to about this. You're the one who seems to actually care about what I feel."

His statement surprised me. I wanted to ask him why he doesn't talk to Hayley about this or why Hayley doesn't care, but then I remembered that she doesn't know about our supernatural being. So instead, I smile back at him and lay my head against his shoulder.

I don't know what caused my actions, especially since I wasn't on speaking terms with him just an hour ago. It just felt like the right thing to do and I wanted to comfort him. In fact, I was tired of fighting with him and bickering. Why couldn't we just be civil?

"Weston, can we be civil? Can we be friends? I'm so tired of fighting." I sighed, waving my white flag. Being friends was better than nothing

Weston's blue eyes widened, before a full-blown smile stretched across his face. "I'm tired of fighting too, Danny. Friends," He said, sticking out his hand to shake.

"Friends," I smiled, feeling a huge weight lift off my shoulders.

There was one thing I've always wanted to talk to about Weston for a long time now. I've been itching to ask him even before I came to Huntstown. It was a question that haunted the both of us, I'm sure.

"What about Warren?" I asked cautiously. I saw him stiffen beside me. "Have you visited him?"

When I moved to live with the Wrode family, I had nightmares every night. I was suffering post traumatic stress from the events that happened that night. I remember screaming in the middle of the night, my relatives barging in with wide eyes.

The wolfs bane would be fresh in my nose. The sight of my mother and Stacey flashed beneath my closed lids, their blood and bruises visible on their dirty skin. My father wanted to kill me, the cold blade pressing into my skin. My dad about to plunge a knife into my mother's heart. My dad dying. Warren wanted to kill my mate.

It was a lot to handle, being in a situation like that for the first time.

I genuinely wanted to know how Warren was. Last thing I heard about him was that he was in a facility, getting better. Apparently, he wasn't in his state of mind when he attacked us.

"He's going to be in the facility for another year before they release him," Weston said, scratching the back of his neck.

"Do you know why he went crazy?"

"He was injected with a type of herbal from an ancient book when he was depressed. This lets you turn off your human feelings, but it is also very dangerous. It causes your animalistic side to dominate and your negative emotions to enhance."

"Why were his parents killed?" I asked him, looking at him with a torn expression. "Healers don't just kill werewolves without valid reasons."

"That's why I didn't want to kill Healers, Danny. They didn't do anything wrong. Warren's parents harmed many people to get a cure for Warren's dad. He was suffering from a huge sickness that was going to kill him soon. Due to the many fatalities, they were subject to die."

I just nodded and I felt bad for Warren. He was depressed and he was acting on a drug. He wasn't in his right state of mind and his parents were fighting for each other. Of course he would think it was the right thing to do to try and heal each other. He loved his parents and he had to lose them. He became depressed.

"Have you visited him?" I asked Weston, laying my head on his shoulder again.

After a couple of seconds, Weston sighed and said, "No. I'm scared." There was a pang in my chest because of how broken he sounded. "He's my best friend and I hate seeing him so weak. He tried to kill me and I know it wasn't on purpose. I knew he was angry because I didn't do anything about his parent's death. I should have done something. At least tell him what his parent's did. He doesn't know about his parent's killing humans. What kid wants to hear that their amazing and super hero parents killed about fifty people?"

I stiffened when I heard this information. So Warren didn't know the truth? That made more sense.

"I always wanted to visit him, but I just can't bring myself to see him," Weston said.

I studied him and I knew that if my best friend was sick, I'd be scared to visit too. So I smiled and nudged his arm with my elbow. "Come on, we're going to visit him tomorrow. You need to see him. I know it's a huge weight on his shoulders to know that he did this to his best friend. You need to find closure."

"Danny, no – "

"We're going, Weston."

"But – "

"No buts. I will drag you if I have to."

"I don't – "

"It's not a good idea, but it's for the best."

"What about you? You're not fine with this, are you?"

"Yes, I'm okay with it," I lied.

"Please, Danny. I don't – "

"You have to go sometime. Might as well go now."

After contemplating, Weston sighed. "Fine."

Although I was scared to see Warren myself, I had to find my closure with him as well.

Chapter 10

The Experts Mental Institute was situated near a lake in a private property. The leaves were beginning to yellow. This area was clean and polished considering it was an institute for the mentally disturbed.

The building was perfectly painted a warm beige color with its name written in black across the front entrance. It was fairly big, standing at three stories high. Brown curtains covered glass windows.

Weston had told me this was one of the two Expert Mental Institutes in Michigan. We were lucky it was only a forty-five minute drive from Huntstown. Weston also informed me that these institutes were in private places and all werewolf doctors here did have a degree.

Weston and I stared at the building for a few minutes longer before I muttered, "Are you ready?"

"Nope. I was never ready. You dragged me here," Weston said, turning back to face my Land Rover. "Why don't we go back home? Warren's probably sleeping. I don't want to disturb him."

"No, we're doing this and if we have to stay here for a whole night for you to finally go inside, then we will."

Weston groaned, stuffing his hands in his leather jacket. "Why are you so stubborn?"

"I've always been stubborn," I smirked, pulling my knit beanie over my head. "I'm here, Weston. I'll help you."

While Weston stared at the building again with fear, I slipped my hand into his warm one. I didn't miss the tingles that ignited in every cell of my body. "Come on, you could do this," I smiled up at him.

We started walking towards the entrance and I was pretty sure Weston hand was starting to sweat. I couldn't blame him. I was scared and nervous to see the person who tried to kill us.

The double doors slid open and the lady at the front desk smiled warmly at us. Her black hair was pulled up into a bun and her brown eyes calculated us. "Hello," she called out.

"Hi," I said when Weston didn't say anything. "We're looking for Warren Greene."

"Mr. Greene has a lot of friends," the woman said with enthusiasm while digging in a drawer. She pulled out a clipboard and a pen. "Please just sign in here and before you leave, you must sign out."

I nodded, signing my name in and practically forcing Weston to sign his name. After we signed in, the lady instructed us to go to the second floor, turn right, and find room number two hundred six. I muttered a thank you and dragged Weston along with me.

"I don't think I could do this," Weston said, pacing inside the elevator while tugging at his black hair.

"Weston, calm down," I said, grabbing his hand and walking onto the second floor. The white linoleum floors were shiny under the fluorescent light. There was the smell of werewolf everywhere mixed in with a slight trace of vanilla. The doors were a dark mahogany, numbers painted on the wood.

He was breathing hard and I had to stop to look at him. "Look, I'm nervous too," I said slowly. It was true. My heart was pounding against my rib cage and the memories of him flashed through my head. I forced the vile images out of my head. Warren was better now. I just knew it.

"So, why are you doing this?" Weston whisper yelled. "Let's just go."

"Give your best friend a chance," I said, comfortingly. He still looked unconvinced, so I tugged his hand in front of Warren's door.

I could hear the television on a football game. My heart was pounding and I tightened my hold on Weston's hand. Weston stood close behind me and I could feel his nervousness. I jumped slightly when I heard a familiar male cheer for his team – a voice I haven't heard in months.

"We could do this," I said, glancing over my shoulder to look at Weston. He looked down, before nodding slowly.

I twisted the knob, opening the door slowly and tugging Weston behind me. Warren was in his bed, which was pushed to one side of the room. A lamp was on a nightstand right next to bed. Under the window was a desk with a few notebooks and pencils. A dresser and a closet was side by side. To the immediate right of us was the door leading to the bathroom.

We walked in a little bit for Warren to see us. When his brown eyes met ours, it widened into saucers. His mouth opened to say something, but nothing came out. His posture stiffened and there a million apologies written in his brown orbs.

"Hey, Warren," I said, smiling when nobody said anything. I gave him a small wave.

"I'm dreaming," he said, running his hand in his brown hair before pinching himself.

"No, you're not," I laughed.

After a couple of minutes of staring at us, Warren hung his head and started crying. His shoulders moved up and down and he tried to muffle his sobs down. He looked up at us with tear-filled eyes. "You guys don't realize how much I'm so sorry," he said. "I'm so, immensely, truly sorry for what I did. There are no excuses for my bad behavior. It was wrong and I don't expect you guys to forgive me, but I'm sorry."

I smiled widely at him, my own tears rolling down my cheeks. I looked up to see Weston with a serious expression, staring at Warren. He still hasn't said anything.

"Gosh, I'm such a pussy," Warren said, rubbing furiously at his tears. I laughed lightly at him. "I'm so sorry. I shouldn't have done that to you, Danny. I really shouldn't. I'm not going to try to make up excuses because that would just make me feel so much worse. Weston, I'm so sorry too. I'm sorry I turned my back on the one person who has been there for me this whole time. I'm sorry I had such negative thoughts on my best friend. I just lost more when I did what I did."

"No, I'm sorry," Weston said for the first time, before giving him a small smile. "I should've done more to help you. I'm also sorry that it took me so long to come visit you."

"I didn't expect you to come. I thought you guys hated me," Warren said, standing up from his bed.

"We don't hate you," I said, before flinging my arms around Warren. I suddenly felt bad for him with everything that Weston told me yesterday. "We just want to help."

Warren cried into my hair a little longer before mumbling apologies repeatedly. I patted his back, telling him it was okay. When we parted, I smiled widely when Weston and Warren did the man hug thing, patting each other's back hard.

"Man, I've missed you," Warren said when he stood in front of us.

"Hey," Weston said, slapping Warren on the back. "I've got to ask you a serious question though."

"What is it?" Warren asked. "Anything. I'll try to answer to the best of my abilities."

"Do you know anything about the hunters that are trying to attack us?" Weston said, looking seriously at Warren. Warren's eyes showed it all. Confusion. "Don't lie to us, Warren. If you do, you will be sentence to death for planning a second attack on werewolves."

"Weston," I gasped, looking at him sternly.

"No, it's okay, Danny," Warren smiled, before turning to look at Weston. "I really don't know what's going on. The only person I've ever talked to about attacking people was Danny's dad. There's an attack?"

"Okay, don't worry about that," I told him, pushing him towards his bed.

"Are you lying?" Weston said, ignoring my glares. He crossed his arms over his chest.

"Wes, I know it's hard to trust me with everything that happened. It's understandable. I'm telling the truth when I say I don't know what is going on. I swear to God."

After a few more questioning from an unconvinced Weston, I interrupted. "So, how are you?" I asked.

Weston took a seat on a chair near the bed while I sat on Warren's bed. Weston leaned forward, concerned over his friend's health.

"Good," Warren said enthusiastically. "They've put me on some medications to drain out those herbs and I feel like a new man. Stacey and I are on the right track and I'm happy. I'm happy that you guys are here too."

"That's good," Weston said.

"The only thing I don't like is the assignments they let us do. It's cheesy."

"Painting and coloring? I saw your smiley face out in the whole. Good effort," Weston laughed.

"You've always been jealous of my artistic skills, Marshall."

I smiled when I saw the two best friends joking around. Weston slapped Warren across the head and Warren put Weston in a headlock. It was refreshing to see that they were going to be ... all right. Weston wasn't going to completely trust him and I wasn't going to completely trust him either. By being here, we were trying to find closure on what had happened that night and we were accomplishing that task.

After a few more minutes of small talk, visiting hours for the afternoon period was over. Weston and I piled into my Land Rover, looking at the building with small smiles on our faces.

"I still don't trust him," Weston sighed.

"I don't either," I said. "But it's a start. It was nice seeing you joke around with him."

"Yeah, it was just like old times before he started getting depressed."

"He's getting better. I could see it."

"So how did you feel going in there?" Weston asked, slouching in his seat.

"I was scared, actually. I think I was as scared as you."

"I wasn't scared," Weston defended, puffing out his chest slightly.

"I had to practically drag you in the room."

"If it were for other reasons, I wouldn't mind going in a room with you," Weston joked, throwing a wink my way. Although I laughed at that, I punched his chest.

"This friendship thing is getting to your head, Dot."

"Oh, so the old nickname comes back!" Weston hollered, rolling down his window and sticking his head out. "It must be a miracle," he yelled to the sky. "She is no longer the rampaging woman on her menopause!"

I hit him again and he laughed. "I'm kidding, Ells," he said, smiling at me. I couldn't help the smile that graced my face too.

It was nice talking and laughing with Weston again.

It probably wasn't going to always be easy like this, but again, it was a start.

We just stared at each other smiling before Weston took me in his muscled arms. "Thanks, Ells," He whispered. "I mean it."

Chapter 11

"Hilatu mikatu," I muttered repeatedly, poising my hands over Beau's palm. Inhaling deeply, I concentrated on the task at hand. I opened my eyes to look at Beau's hand, groaning in disappointment. "Why can't I get this right?"

I dropped my hands onto my thighs with a loud slap, throwing my head back in frustration.

"Don't beat yourself up, Danny," Beau encouraged. "Just try again."

"You're practically bleeding to death because of me," I muttered pointedly, sighing when I saw Beau's frightened face.

We were in the kitchen, practicing my healing abilities. Fourteen months of training and I still haven't perfected my powers. Every time I tried, I would fail miserably while Beau's wound would get worse with every attempt.

It would usually go like this: Beau would randomly train me. He'd take a knife and cut a small slash on his palm. Before it would heal due to his werewolf abilities, I'd start with what I was taught. I would recite the words, "hilatu mikatu" repeatedly with my eyes closed, trying to get in touch with nature. I don't even know what language those two words were from, but I do know in English, it meant healing. When I'd open my eyes, Beau's wound would be bigger, bleed more, or get deeper. Obviously, that was far from being healed.

That meant only one thing.

I failed.

And I kept failing.

"Just try again," Beau urged again, looking at his bloody hand. "You'll get it eventually."

"Are you sure? You just don't want to stop now?" I asked, knitting my eyebrows in concern. He literally looked like he was in pain. Every time I'd ask him how it felt, he'd lie and say it didn't feel like anything. However, I knew it was either stinging, burning, or aching.

"I'm fine. Let's just continue," Beau reassured, holding his bloody hand out to me. He wiped off blood with the third napkin he used today.

"Okay," I said after a couple of seconds. I closed my eyes, poising my hand over his palm. Inhaling, I recited, "Hilatu mikatu. Hilatu mikatu. Hilatu mikatu. Hilatu mikatu. Hilatu mikatu ..."

I opened my eyes and groaned once more. The wound was leaking out blood.

"Hilatu mikatu," I concentrated. "Hilatu mikatu, hilatu mikatu, hilatu mikatu..."

I felt like crying when once again, it didn't work. Banging my head onto the table, I whined. "I'm such a useless Healer!"

"You are not," Beau scolded, wiping blood off his hand. "Never say a Healer is useless, even if you are talking about yourself."

"How come I always fail? You got it in a few weeks, so how come it's taking me so long?" I complained, getting mad at myself for constantly failing.

"You just need to find yourself," Beau said. "Maybe it isn't your time yet. You need to get in touch with nature. You need to put down the wall that's between the both of you."

"What the hell? How do you do that?"

"I don't know," Beau screamed back, frightened by my anger. He looked funny with his brown eyes widening and his shoulders going up. "I never had to go through that! I'm sorry."

"I feel so stupid! You keep teaching me and I never learn from my mistakes! I'm sorry, Beau," I said, tugging at my long brown hair.

"Come on," Beau sighed, putting his hand in front of me. "Let's try this one more time."

"Fine," I huffed, closing my eyes. I concentrated hard, calling out to nature. "Hilatu mikatu, hilatu mikatu, hilatu mikatu…"

Still bleeding.

"Hilatu mikatu. Hilatu mikatu. Hilatu mikatu. Hilatu mik – "

"What the hell are you doing to Beau?" A male voice shouted, breaking my concentration.

I opened my eyes and groaned. Turning around to glare at the ginger, I crossed my arms over my chest.

"Why are you killing him?" Jet yelled at me, looking at Beau's hand with wide eyes. Beau just smirked, amused by the situation. "And what the fuck are you saying? Is it some type of witchcraft? I've always known you were evil!"

"Gee, thanks Jet," I replied sarcastically. "I was practicing my Healer abilities by the way."

Jet's eyebrows knitted together, scrutinizing Beau's bloody hand and the three bloody napkins next to him. His eyebrows shot up before he looked at me. "Uh, you're doing a great job, Danny!" He lied. Jet was always a bad liar. He threw a thumb up in my direction before heading out the door.

"Okay, let's continue," Beau encouraged, sticking his hand in front of me.

"I think we should take a break. I'm not feeling it anymore."

"Danny, you'll get it someday. I'm fine. If you want to practice some more, I'm more than willing to help you out.

"Beau, I'm not in the mood anymore," I said disappointedly, avoiding his penetrating gaze. "I don't want that wound to worsen especially with my added negativity."

"Don't give up."

"I'm not giving up. I'm just taking a break. I'm sure I'd get it sooner or later," I said, trying to convince him. It sounded like I was trying to convince myself as well.

"Okay. Well, I'm just going to clean this up and cook something. Do you want anything?"

I shook my head, getting up and walking up the stairs. I decided to ask Weston about what the hunters and rogues want as part of our investigation.

After convincing Beau that I would be fine talking to Weston by myself, he gave in and agreed to the idea.

I was confident that Weston would share the information with me because we were on speaking terms. He always used to tell me things that dealt with werewolf business. Therefore, I decided to give it a shot and ask him.

"Weston," I called when I knocked on his bedroom door. "It's Danny!"

There was no response. I was sure he was home. His car was parked in the garage and he would have announced his departure, telling us to call him if anything went wrong.

"Weston," I called again, knocking on the door continually.

When there was no response, I opened his bedroom door slowly. His scent crashed into me. Unintentionally, I let out a low moan. It was tidy and it was empty.

A king sized bed with white bed sheets was pushed up again one beige wall. A small leather couch and a single beanbag was situated in front of a hanging, flat screen television. The window across the room was draped with white curtains. Underneath the window was a desk with several papers scattered along the surface and a laptop in the middle. To the left were two doors that led to his bathroom and his closet.

Before I could close the door and leave, something on his nightstand caught my eye. I walked in, shutting the door behind me and walking over to the picture frame. I scrutinized it with my eyebrows drawn together in confusion.

In the middle of the black, intricate border was a picture of Weston and me. My arms were around his neck, hugging him from behind. My smile was wide as he kissed me on the cheek. We were messing around and Jade decided to take a picture of us with her DSLR camera.

I was beyond confused.

Why did he have our photo on his nightstand? Doesn't Hayley come in here? Has she seen this photo? What the hell was that foul smell?

I scrunched up my nose when I caught a slight trace of something tainted. If I were a regular werewolf, I wouldn't have caught the scent. Being a Healer, everything was heightened.

Why did it smell so familiar?

I decided to take a big inhale of the air around me. Despite Weston's delicious scent, that slight trace was disturbing. My wolf was prancing around me. Before I knew it, my feet were moving around the room while I tried to find out where it was coming from.

I knew it was wrong snooping around Weston's stuff, but the scent was bugging me.

I bet down near Weston's bed where the scent was much stronger. I resisted the urge to gag. Looking under his bed, I saw something wrapped in a bunch of Weston's clothes. I pulled out the pile of clothes and put it in front of me.

When Weston's clothes were in a neat pile next to me, a huge black box was facing me. The smell was stronger now, causing my eyes to water at it's stench. I opened the box slowly.

Then I threw it across the room, staring at it with horror-stricken eyes. My hand was trembling as I brought it up to cover my open mouth.

Why did Weston have a rifle, a case of a hundred wolfs bane-laced bullets, and a wolfs bane laced spear?

Before I could hide any evidence that I was there and run out as quickly as possible, the door opened. Weston stood before me, observing the weapons in the corner.

"Danny," Weston asks cautiously, looking at me with intense eyes. "What are you doing in my room?"

Chapter 12

Not edited!

Enjoy! (:

"Danny, it's not what it looks like," Weston said slowly as I glared at him.

Hot tears were streaming down my flushed face. I was angry. Scratch that. I was furious. What the hell was he doing with those vile weapons?

There were many questions popping up in my head, but I couldn't bring myself to speak it out loud. Maybe I was assuming things. I don't know, but actually possessing those weapons instead of throwing it out did not make sense for a werewolf.

"Enlighten me, Weston," I said angrily. I motioned my hand towards the weapons in the corner. "Why the hell do you have those?"

"Calm down," Weston said cautiously, putting his hands up and walking towards me.

"Don't touch me," I stepped back. Weston flinched, returning his arms to his side.

"Why do you have it?" I asked once again.

"I have it because I found it during the attack," Weston sighed. "I didn't want anyone to find out about it – "

"Why not?" I snapped.

"Because they were going to freak out like what you're doing right now and they wouldn't hesitate to throw it out," Weston answered.

"Why do you have it?"

"I've been trying to find a way to avoid being affected by these things when the hunters and rogues attack. I've been searching in every ancient book and talking to every elder, but I haven't found anything," Weston said tiredly.

I felt my anger diminish as I heard his reason for possessing the rifle, bullets, and a spear. Turns out, it wasn't only Beau and I doing our separate investigations. I sat down next to Weston, contemplating whether I should tell him what Beau and I had found out.

I chose not to. Beau wouldn't be too happy with me if I shared out information with Weston out of all people.

"I'm sorry," I said after a couple of seconds. "I shouldn't have assumed the worst."

"It's normal. Everyone does, right?" Weston smiled tightly. "Anyways, what are you doing in my room?"

I laughed nervously. "Well, I came here to ask you a question, but something caught my eye and I went to look at it. I'm nosy, I know. I've always been. That's when I caught a whiff of the wolfs bane. You know, Healers have enhanced senses. I was being nosy again. I'm sorry. I shouldn't have – " Weston cut off my babbling.

"What caught your eye?" He asked, his blue eyes burning with curiosity.

I felt the blood rush to my cheeks. "W-well, I found that," I stumbled to get the words out, pointing at the picture frame.

I might be imagining things, but I swore Weston's cheek had the slightest tint of pink. He scratched the back of his neck. "Oh," Weston said after a while.

"Yeah," I said awkwardly when he didn't explain further.

I really wanted to know why he still had it. I mean, he did have a girl friend. Wasn't he scared that Hayley was going to find it? Sure, I had a picture of us, but he had a girl friend now.

"So, what did you want to ask me?" He digressed.

"Okay, so I was wondering," I clapped my hands together and got down to business. "What do the hunters and rogues want? What's that important?"

Weston's face fell and he clenched his jaw. His posture stiffened. "I'm sorry, but I can't tell you."

"Why not?" I shot up to my feet, placing my hands on my hips.

"Only Jarred and I know. It's classified information. It's better if nobody else knew," Weston explained. "Please just leave it at that."

"I want to help!" I yelled. "I feel so useless sitting here!"

"You're not useless," Weston said calmly. "You didn't change, did you? You're still nosy, demanding, angry, stubborn, and a little psycho," he joked, smirking.

"I'm serious!" I slapped his chest lightly.

"You're still violent," Weston ignored my serious expression, listing down more of my negative features. "You're pushy. You're controlling. You're –
"

"Okay, shut up," I said flatly.

"Why are you so serious all the damn time? You're like an old librarian who owns twenty cats. I haven't seen you really enjoy life. You know what you need?" Weston got up from his bed, looking at me with mischievous eyes.

"What?" I asked slowly, stepping back when he walked closer to me.

He smirked evilly before quickly grabbing my hips in his hands and tickling me. "You need to laugh," Weston yelled in between my laughter.

"S-stop," I managed to gasp out in between laughter. My embarrassing hiccups followed each giggle. I haven't laughed like this in a long time.

It felt good.

"Ah, I missed that laugh," Weston chuckled as I struggled to escape his hands.

"W-Weston," I screamed when he squeezed my side.

"That's right," Weston joked. "Scream my name."

"You're such a perv," I choked out, slapping his chest. When he squeezed my side once more, my leg jerked causing an accidental kick to his nuts.

His hands immediately left my side, clutching his crotch. He groaned in pain, falling to the ground. I watched shortly with wide eyes, before bursting into a fit of giggles.

"Oh my gosh," I gasped between my laughter and hiccups. I clutched my tummy, literally crying in amusement. "That's what you get, Dot!"

"You're going to pay for that," Weston grunted, slowly getting up. I watched with horror, before running away. I squealed, locking the bathroom door before he could push it open.

"I have the key, you know," Weston said through the door. "This is war!"

"You're so immature," I yelled back.

His showerhead was big and the removable type. An idea popped into my head before I laughed mischievously. I stepped into the tub, grabbing the showerhead in my hands and getting ready for my remarkable attack.

"I'm coming in," Weston yelled. I heard the key jingling and the doorknob turning.

When the door opened, I let out an Indian cry before turning the water on and spraying him. His face was priceless. His blue eyes widened and his mouth flew open in surprise. He put his arms in front of him.

"I'm the immature one? You're making my whole bathroom wet!" He cried.

I turned the water off while giggling. He stood there with his arms crossed over his chest. He was dripping wet, his thin t-shirt clinging to his muscles. His black hair was flat against his head and tiny drops of water were dripping off his chin. I would have drooled at the sight of him, but he was ready to attack.

After staring at each other for a couple of minutes, Weston said, "You're going to regret that." I dropped the showerhead in shock when he used his inhuman speed and climbed in the huge bathtub with me. Before I could grab it, he took it in his hands and turned it on. I squealed as the cold water pierced my skin.

Weston's laughter was cut short when I grabbed his delicious smelling shampoo and squirted it at him. He let go of the showerhead when the shampoo was about to drip into his eyes.

"That's expensive shampoo!" Weston complained.

I stuck my tongue out at him, wringing my green sweater. "You asked for it," I yelled childishly.

Weston sprayed me with the showerhead once more and I gave him a menacing glare. "You don't play fair," he whined. I laughed when he almost slipped.

Before I could pick up his shampoo bottle again, he pinned me against the wall and grabbed the bottle in his hand. He squirted it on my skin. It was starting to get sticky with every second my skin was drying.

He started tickling me again and I hiccupped. "Okay, stop," I gasped. "I give up. Truce?"

Weston's hands stopped on my hips, but he made no move to remove it. His smirk grew into my favorite genuine smile as his blue eyes pierced into mine. I tried not to blush when I realized our bodies were flushed against each other.

"Although you wasted perfectly good and expensive shampoo, we should call a truce," Weston joked. "You smell like me."

"I stink," I joked too, wrinkling my nose.

Weston scoffed, but he didn't say anything. He just picked up a hand and softly pushed a wet strand of hair behind my ear. I almost closed my eyes from pleasure, but I didn't want to miss the way his blue irises were piercing into mine.

In that moment, I forgot all my problems and I felt human. Weston was the only person who could make me feel like a normal human. Although he was my mate, my wolf would leave me alone when we were in the presence of Weston. She would be too busy bonding with Weston's wolf. Even if it were just a couple of minutes, I basked in humanity.

Hayley flashed in my head. No girl deserved to be cheated on and I wasn't about to wreck Weston and Hayley's relationship.

I picked up my hand and trailed it down the side of his face. I didn't miss the way his head tilted closer to my hand, the way he gulped, and the way he looked at me with pain, passion, longing, and a ton of other emotions flashing in his blue eyes. Placing my hand flat on his cheek, I smiled at him.

"I think I should go," I said, swallowing the tears.

Stepping out of the tub, I exited his bedroom with my heart aching.

Chapter 13

I was so bored.

Jet, Stacey, and I groaned simultaneously, causing Stacey to giggle.

Beau was out with Darren doing fun things. I knew they went paintballing, go carting, and skiing. When I asked if I could go, Darren looked guilty. He was trying to find excuses as to why I couldn't tag along. Beau bluntly told me this was a "man" day and they didn't want any females to interrupt them.

Apparently, they thought females were always burdens to what men considered fun. I simply stuck my tongue out at them and said they were jerks. Kelly did the same, glaring at Darren.

Elliot, Abigail, Jade, and Jarred went on a double date run. They asked if we wanted to go, but we turned their offer down nicely. We didn't want to feel left out.

It also made us envy their perfect relationship.

After all, my mate had a human girl friend. Stacey's mate was in a mental institute. Jet didn't find his mate yet. We were completely lucky when it came to the romance department.

Note the sarcasm.

Weston was doing some Alpha duties upstairs, so that left the three of us moaning about how bored we were. We seriously had no life.

"How's Warren?" Jet asked after thinking about a topic to discuss.

"Fine," Stacey answered, throwing her platinum blonde hair out of her face. Her sapphire eyes showed concern over her mate. "He's doing so much better."

"That's great," Jet said sincerely. "I haven't visited in such a long time. I'll go soon."

"Danny visited," Stacey said with enthusiasm. "She went with Weston!"

"You went with Weston?" Jet asked with one eyebrow quirking up. "How'd you get him to go? And what happened to the war of the exes?"

Stacey punched him, casting him a warning look. I waved it off and just sighed.

"I practically dragged him there. We're fine. We called a truce," I said. "I think he's going to visit Warren again soon."

"Thank you, Danny," Stacey gleamed. "Warren has been beating himself up over what he did to you and Weston. As far as I know, he will never forgive himself for the rest of his life. When you visited, it was a huge weight off his shoulders."

"It was for the best," I smiled, playing with Jet's rusted color hair. "So I can't help my curiosity, how are the two of you?"

"We haven't mated yet," Stacey said. "He's in a mental institute. It's kind of weird to get it on in – "

"Okay, we get it," Jet said, covering his ears with his hands. "Nasty. I have more than enough with Eli and Abigail."

"Anyways," Stacey said, glaring at Jet. "We're just dating. That's all."

"I'm lucky I haven't found my mate," Jet sighed.

"What? You don't want to find true love?" I asked. Jet always seemed like the person who constantly looked for true love. I guess I thought wrong.

"It's so complicated," Jet groaned, looking at me like it was the most obvious thing in the world. "Femme wolves are such bitches."

Stacey smacked his head. "You better watch it, Cavanaugh," Stacey defended the female population.

"See," Jet yelled, motioning a hand towards Stacey's angry face. "Bitch."

"You're really mean," I told him. "Maybe that's because you're already nineteen and your heart is becoming colder every day you don't have a mate."

"That's not true," Jet replied bitterly. He was lying. He was longing for a mate. He just didn't want to let us know because he was ashamed of his vulnerability.

"So, you're saying that if you found a mate, you would reject her?" Stacey asked.

"No," Jet answered quickly. "I would not let her go through that."

"Ah, so you have thought of finding your mate. You already know you'd welcome her with open arms," I teased, ruffling his hair.

He rolled his chocolate eyes. "I'm just a gentleman, that's all."

"I didn't know gentlemen called females bitches," Stacey replied sarcastically.

"I'm one in a million, sweetheart. By the way, Danny, what exactly is going on with you and Weston?"

"Nothing. We're friends," I shrugged.

"Just friends? How is that going for you?" Stacey asked with curious eyes.

"Okay, I guess. It's going to be hard, but at least we were civil. Making him my enemy is too much drama."

"I hate to bring it up, but Weston is obviously hiding some things from you," Jet said. Stacey gulped, averting her eyes. Weston had many secrets so I wasn't completely surprised.

My eyebrows rose and I simply asked, "Why do you think that?"

"Well, every time he thinks he ends the link with us, he starts muttering things about you," Jet stated. "Right, Stace?"

Stacey nodded. My eyebrows knitted in confusion with my lips slightly parted. I didn't know how to respond to that. What was he muttering?

"What does he say?" I asked, contemplating whether I should hear this information or leave it as it is.

"He grumbles to himself about how much he's an idiot. That one's right. He put you through a lot of crap," Jet said. "He'd say things about how he missed you and the other day, he was going on and on about how good it felt to have you in his arms."

"Um," I said awkwardly, feeling the blood rush up to my cheeks. "He wasn't aware that you guys were listening?"

"Sometimes you forget that you haven't put up the link block if something is bothering you," Stacey said, looking at me cautiously. "He talks about you a lot. He'd cuss every time he realized we were listening, but none of us had the courage to ask him what was going on."

"Why would he talk about me?" I asked. I felt the riot of butterflies in my stomach. My heart was pounding against my rib cage.

"You're his mate," Stacey shrugged. "I guess."

"He has a girl friend," I pointed out. "As much as I hate to say this, but I think if he wanted to be with me, he wouldn't be with Hayley right now."

"He loves her," Jet said bluntly. Stacey smacked him across the chest. Unfortunately, that news was clear a long time ago. However, it still dimmed my mood and made me more depressed. "But, I think there is more to the story than Weston is letting on."

"What do you mean?"

"I have no clue either, but I feel like he's hiding stuff," Jet said.

"He's definitely hiding a lot," Stacey agreed, nodding her head. "He's been different lately."

"What do you mean by different?"

"He's been acting weird. He's been more moody and snappy," Jet answered for Stacey.

"Why?"

"Wouldn't we all want to know?"

I sat there, trying to make sense of the information. There were many questions swimming in my head, but I had a feeling that Stacey and Jet didn't have the answers to these. They were as clueless and curious as I was.

"I think he still lo – " Stacey began, but was cut off by the front door banging open.

It was so loud, causing the three of us to jump a foot in the air. We looked at each other in confusion. Our eyes widened when we heard screams of agony, shouting, and the rushing of feet across the tiled floors.

"Something happened," Stacey said worriedly, getting up to her feet. "Jade just linked me."

"What?" I asked, gripping her arm. She just stared at the entrance of the living room with frightened eyes. Her face paled and her lips were muttering words that I could not decipher.

Jet's face was similar to Stacey's own. He got up to his feet as fast as he could. He was about to jump over the couch, when the commotion entered the room.

My eyes widened and the sight in front of me made me dizzy. A loud gasp escaped my lips unintentionally. My hands started to tremble and my body went cold.

Eli rushed into the room shirtless, muttering something to Abigail. Abigail was in his arms, her small body covered in Eli's light blue t-shirt. She convulsed in his arms, screaming in agony. Eli shook, crying as he shouted orders at Jet. Jade tried to whisper comforting words to Jarred whose face was flushed. Tears were streaming out of his eyes. After he punched the wall hard, he tangled his hands in his blonde hair.

Then my eyes flew to Abigail's stomach where dark red blood was soaking the cloth of Eli's t-shirt.

"S-she was s-stabbed," Eli cried, pushing Abigail's hair out of her pale face. "She's dying from the w-wolfs bane."

"Please help her, Danny," Jarred sounded broken, looking at me with bloodshot eyes. "Please heal her."

Chapter 14

IN NEED OF SERIOUS EDITING.

ENJOY! (:

Everyone started yelling. They started shuffling around, grabbing blankets, water, and other necessities. Everything was a big mess, but it was drowned out by the favor that Jarred had asked me.

"Please help her, Danny," Jarred sounded broken, looking at me with bloodshot eyes. "Please heal her."

"Danny, please," Eli pleaded. My chest tightened from how broken he sounded. "Please, I'm begging you."

I hated seeing Abigail like this. She was one of my best friends and I couldn't stand seeing her in so much pain or stand the thought of her dying. I closed my eyes when she coughed, blood spluttering out.

The commotion was much louder now. Everyone was helping as much as they could.

"I'll link Beau," I announced, frightened. "He'll be here quick, trust me."

"We don't have time," Jarred said frustrated, pacing around the living room and getting angrier by the minute. "You have to do it, Danny. She's dying! My sister is dying!"

If I were even a tiny bit good at healing, I would have gave it a shot without thought. The only problem was the fact that I sucked at healing. If I risked it, her injury would have worsened and she would have died because of my mistake. However, if I didn't even try and she died, it would still be my fault.

My head started spinning and my tongue felt like sandpaper. Sweat was spotting on my forehead and my head was pounding. I couldn't do this.

"Please," Beau said breathlessly when Abigail's screams were coming out tiredly.

"What happened?" Weston yelled frantically, running into the room. When he saw the commotion, he threw his hand in his dark hair. "Shit."

"Abigail ran ahead of us to show us something. That's when two hunters came out of the bushes and one stabbed Abigail," Jade supplied with her voice quavering. She cried as she looked down at Abigail. "Eli and Jarred finished the hunters while I tried to aid Abigail. That's when we figured – figured out – that the wound was – was," Jade continued. She couldn't even finish her statement.

"Danny, she's getting weaker," Jarred screamed, motioning his hand towards his sister. "Help."

"I might do it wrong," I replied, feeling guilty. "If I try, it could worsen. I don't want her to die because of my mistake."

"Danny," Weston said, coming over to me and grabbing my head in between his hands. His blue eyes pierced into me. "You could do this. Just concentrate. Please don't just stand there when you're the only one who could do something about it. She's dying, Danny. Just concentrate. Breathe. You could do it."

I looked at Abigail. Her skin was so pale. Her eyes kept rolling back, but Eli refused to let her sleep. She moaned in agony.

I had to do something. I had to try.

"Okay, I'll do it," I whispered, looking into Weston's piercing blue eyes.

"You'll do fine," Weston smiled, letting go of my face.

Everyone went dead silent as I threw orders at them. "Eli, I need you to lay her on the couch. Someone, please get water, a whole roll of napkins, and fresh clothes for Abigail. I also need a first aid kit," I said, feeling much more confident.

Eli placed Abigail on the couch softly. She moaned softly in pain. Jade, Jet, and Stacey placed all the materials next to me in the next minute. Eli grabbed his mate's hand. Jarred stood next to his twin sister, stroking her hair.

Swallowing hard, I ripped the shirt where the wound was. There were a few gasps – including mine – when we saw the deep cut on Abigail's flat stomach. Blood was gushing out of it. The wound was turning black from the wolfs bane.

I tried to calm down as much as possible before I proceeded. I really didn't want to mess up. Instead of thinking about what was going on, I closed my eyes and thought of a positive outcome. I thought of Abigail healthy and glowing, smiling and laughing.

I drew in a shaky breath, placing my hands over the wound. I called for help from the ancient healers as I recited the familiar words and started the healing process.

"Hilatu mikatu. Hilatu mikatu. Hilatu mikatu," I whispered.

I imagined Abigail crying at the altar, smiling widely at Eli. She looked beautiful in her wedding gown.

"Hilatu mikatu. Hilatu mikatu …"

I imagined a wall in between a blooming tree and me. I imagined myself knocking it down and delicately caressing a beautiful, golden leaf.

"Hilatu mikatu …"

I felt an unfamiliar warmth hum through my body, a jolt of electricity ignited in my fingertips.

"Hilatu mikatu. Hilatu mikatu …"

I imagined Abigail telling Eli that she was pregnant. She laughed as Eli picked her up and twirled her around in excitement.

"Hilatu mikatu …"

The tree was glowing. A pure white wolf with a black heart on her forehead appeared, looking at me with proud green eyes.

'You could do this,' my wolf encouraged. 'We were made for this.'

"Hilatu mikatu. Hilatu mikatu…" The words were rolling off my tongue.

I imagined that Abigail, Jade, Stacey, and I went shopping. Abigail always picked out the ugliest things for us to try on. This time, she made me try on a feathery white dress that made me look like a chicken. She laughed with the other girls as I posed for them.

"Hilatu mikatu…"

Abigail and Jarred were playing a game. Abigail won. She rubbed it in her brother's face.

"Hilatu mikatu…"

The golden leaves were circling my wolf. My wolf opened her mouth, sucking in the leaves. Once she was done, it was dark. My wolf stared back at me.

'Open your eyes,' she said with a wolfy grin before she disappeared.

I opened my eyes slowly. The first thing I heard was a soft moan. My eyes widened when Eli and Jarred sobbed harder.

Oh crap, did I fail?

My eyes fell to Abigail's stomach. A thin scar replaced the huge wound.

My heart rate decreased.

A huge smile graced my face.

I leaned back before saying, "I did it. Oh my gosh! I did it!"

I couldn't help it. I jumped to my feet with joy. All of a sudden, I was being pulled into many different hugs. They were praising me for my work. I blushed at all the attention I was receiving.

"Thank you," Eli said, crying tears of relief. I choked from his tight hug. "Thank you so, so, so much."

Jarred pulled me into his arms and I returned his hug. I patted his back comfortingly as he cried into my shoulder. "Thank you so much, D," He mumbled happily. "I don't know what I would have done if my twin sister died. I cannot thank you enough."

"It's okay now," I murmured back, smiling as I spoke the truth. "She'll be fine."

"You were awesome!" Stacey yelled in my ear. I flinched back and laughed at her. "It was beautiful! I swore I saw sparks coming out of your fingertips."

"I saw them too. You did a great job, Danny," Jade said, ruffling my hair.

"I knew she was a witch," Jet joked. "But she wasn't as evil as I thought."

I smacked him across the head. He grinned, but praised me for my work.

"I told you that you could do it," Weston smirked, standing beside me while we watched Eli wipe the blood off Abigail's stomach. "It freaked me out when you started muttering something in alien. I had to be honest, that was kind of unattractive."

I rolled my eyes before smacking his shoulder.

"I'm kidding. You did a great job," he beamed.

"Thanks," I said. "For having faith in me."

Before he could say anything else, Jarred clapped his hands to get everyone's attention. "Guys, Danny officially learned how to heal!"

My friends shouted and clapped. I blushed once again from the attention. I shuffled my feet.

Beau strolled into the living room with a pretzel in his hand. He looked down at Abigail and observed everyone's proud faces. "What did I miss?" He asked, confused.

We laughed at him.

Chapter 15

I N NEED OF MAJOR EDITING.

ENJOY!

DON'T HATE ME TOO MUCH.

MUAH

Abigail was doing much better. She was a little sore and she had a fever, but her health was improving gradually due to her werewolf abilities. She felt like she owed me her whole life, but it wasn't in my best interest to look for something in return. I was the type to do favors for people because it was right – not because I was looking for a grand prize at the end of every good deed done.

Beau was proud of me for discovering a way to connect with my healing abilities. His training had also become more challenging. However, I succeeded at most of the tasks he gave to me.

I've also discovered a new ability.

I tried it out on Abigail and her fever had gone down gradually. Beau was practically jumping up and down in excitement at my rare power. Apparently, I had the ability to better an illness, but only to a certain extent.

After the thousandth time of reciting the words repeatedly, my throat was as dry as sand paper. I ended our training and headed for the kitchen.

I went straight for the cupboard, reaching up on my tiptoes. In times like this, I cursed my short height. I smiled in victory when the glass cup was safely in my hands.

"Hey," a female greeted out of nowhere. I jumped a foot in the air, startled. I turned around, clutching the glass to my chest.

"Oh, hey," I said awkwardly when I saw Hayley sitting at the kitchen table on her cell phone.

"Sorry I scared you," Hayley apologized, putting her phone down.

"Oh, no," I waved off. "I just didn't see you there. I was focused on getting myself a drink. My throat is as dry as the Sahara desert. Would you like something to drink?"

"No, thank you," Hayley said politely. "I'm just waiting for Weston to come down."

I sit down on the seat across from her. Although it was extremely awkward, it was rude for me to leave Hayley here by herself. I took a sip of my water, feeling the cool liquid slide down my dry throat.

Hayley's phone dinged, slicing through the awkward silence like a knife.

"Sorry," she said, lowering the volume of her phone. "I'm texting my mother. It's been a long time since I've talked to her. My parents are divorced."

I was quite shocked with how easy it came from her lips. She didn't seem the slightest bit embarrassed that her parents weren't together anymore.

"It's alright," I said. "You should talk to your mom. I'm sorry to hear about your parents' divorce."

"My parents were divorced too," I added when Hayley didn't say anything. It surprised me that I was being open with her. I guess it was because we had something in common and it was the only thing to talk about. I'd rather say the most embarrassing things than sit here and stare at her while there was an awkward silence between the both of us.

"They were? So they got back together?" Hayley asked, folding her arms on top of the table.

"Not quite," I said, shaking my head. I couldn't believe I was sharing so much of my life with this stranger. "My dad died about fifteen months ago."

Hayley's eyes widened, her lips frowning. She was pitying me. I usually hated being pitied, but I've gotten used to it. "I'm so sorry, Danny," Hayley said sincerely.

"I still don't know how to respond to that," I answered honestly, laughing. "I don't know whether to say 'it's okay', 'thank you', or 'I'm fine'. Nothing relatively fits."

"Tell me about it," Hayley laughed too. "Every time I hear that, I don't know what to say."

"So, you live with your dad?" I asked.

"Yup," she says, popping the p. "They divorced when I was eleven. Ever since then, I stayed with my dad. I would talk to my mother occasionally.

Usually, I visit her at New York City over the summer. I love small towns. Big cities overwhelm me."

"I used to live in the city," I laughed. "I moved to this small town two years ago. Fourteen months ago, I moved to another small town with relatives. I kind of like cities. They keep you busy. It helps you forget all the problems you're having. I'm attached to Huntstown though."

"I grew up here," Hayley explains. "All my family and friends are here. I'm afraid of letting that go."

"You must have a great family," I smiled.

"So, forgive me for asking, but why did your parents have a divorce? You don't have to answer if it makes you uncomfortable."

I pursed my lips. After a couple of seconds, I simply say, "He found out some things he wasn't supposed to and found a whore half his age."

"Oh," Hayley exclaims. "That's tough!"

"What about your parents?"

"Reconcilable differences." Hayley smiled. "They just lost feelings for each other."

"Oh," I simply said. It must be hard for a kid to see their parents divorce just because they actually didn't love each other. "Are you an only child?"

"Yes. What about you?"

"I have an older brother. He's twenty one. He got married when he was only twenty, but he's pretty sure that she's the one," I said proudly. It was always second nature for me to brag about Darren.

"That's cute," Hayley smiled genuinely. "What about your mom? What is she like?"

"She's wonderful," I said honestly. "She's truly a super mom. She does everything for us. She owns her own business. She's a fashion designer."

My mom does truly do everything for Darren and I. She would literally take bullets for us. Talking about her made me want to cry. I was proud to be her daughter.

"That's so cool," Hayley exclaimed. "My dad owns a business too, but it's just a small shop in town."

"What store?" I asked, sipping my water.

"The Big Shot," Hayley replied. I choked on my water, looking at Hayley with wide eyes. "Yeah, I know. He sells guns for a living. It's something I'm not so proud about."

"Your dad is Henry?" I asked alarmed.

"You know him?" Hayley asked suspiciously.

"Yeah, I mean, I've heard about him around town. I heard he's a sharp shooter," I lied.

Did Weston know Hayley's dad was a hunter? Did he know he was the one who created those vile weapons? If Hayley found out what we were, we'd be dead in a second. Would she nark on her boy friend? Was she undercover? She seemed sincere and clueless. Why the hell was the world so screwed up?

I'm so confused.

"Yeah, he is pretty good with the guns," Hayley agreed.

"Did Weston meet him yet? I know Weston's into guns," I lied again. I wanted to know if Weston knew what he was getting himself into. I couldn't stand to see him hurt.

"Yeah, Weston and my dad get along pretty well. Weston's my dad's favorite. My dad teaches him how to shoot at the ranch sometimes," Hayley says happily while I was anything but happy.

My palms started getting clammy and my blood ran cold when everything started to click into place. The weapons I found in Weston's room. The shootings he practiced with the one and only creator of the vile weapons – his girl friend's dad. The werewolves that were teaming up with the hunters. The reason why he was putting his pack in danger because "he didn't want to give up something that was excessively valuable". The reason why he didn't want to give me an answer when I asked him what the hunters and rogues wanted. It because he didn't have an answer in the first place. It was all lies.

I felt my fist clench under the table, my heart aching at the hurtful truth. My eye twitched as I replayed the painful discovery in my head. There was no way Weston was betraying us, right?

Maybe I was over thinking the situation. Maybe I was assuming things once again. There was only one way to find out the truth and I knew how I was going to get my answer.

"I should get going," I said, trying to keep my voice even. I plastered a fake smile. "I almost forgot I had a meeting. It was nice talking to you, Hayley. See you, later."

***

"Kid," the familiar raspy voice shouted happily. "Long time no see! Where's your brother?"

Ron beamed at me, fixing the faded blue cap on his head. I smiled back sweetly, putting my hands on the counter. "He's watching my sister," I lied.

"Has he changed his mind?" Ron asked excitedly.

"Nope," I simply said, shrugging my shoulders.

Ron's face fell a little, before he smiled widely again. "So, how can I help you?"

"I was wondering if I could get a list of all the hunters in the group," I said sweetly, praying he wouldn't ask any questions.

Today just wasn't my day.

"Why?" Ron asked suspiciously, his furry eyebrows knitting together.

I mentally groaned. He was making this harder than it was supposed to me. My fake smile grew wider.

"Well," I stalled, trying to find a good excuse. "My brother and I are planning something and I don't want to ruin the surprise."

"Surprise?" Ron asked like a child on Christmas. He was so gullible. I almost wanted to laugh at him.

"Yup," I winked. "We really appreciate what you men do. You risk your lives for the citizens of this town."

Gag.

"Oh," Ron smiled bigger, jumping up and down in excitement. I knew what he was thinking. He actually thought that we were going to do something special for them. "Well, I'll be back. I'll print out the names for you."

I waited impatiently as he printed the names. I paced around the front, feeling my stomach clench uncomfortably. Should I go home and mind my own business?

Hell no. We all know how stubborn and nosy I was.

"Here you go," Ron said cheerfully, placing the sheet of paper in my sweaty hands. I muttered a thank you, holding the paper that held all my answers with a light grip. It felt like a ticking bomb in my hand. Walking out the front door, Ron yelled, "We'll see you soon, kid!"

I rolled my eyes.

Climbing into my Land Rover, I closed my eyes and drew in a shaky breath. This was it. My hands were trembling as I read the list of names on the white sheet of paper.

Henry Price

Ronald Higgins

Paul Kearny

Samuel Walker

Fred Abbot

Weston Marshall

I threw the sheet of paper with disgust and shock, tasting the bile in my throat.

Chapter 16

ENJOY!

Without knocking on Weston's door, I barge in angrily. He looked annoyed, turning his head away from his television show. His eyes widened and he stood up when he saw it was I.

"Danny, what's wro –"

His words were cut short with the sharp slap that caused his head to whip to the left. The contact was so loud, slicing the calm atmosphere like a knife. Although it was a solid slap, it did nothing to release the pent up anger burning inside of me.

It was silent. Weston's head was still whipped to the left with his mouth slightly open. Shock was clear in his blue eyes. His cheek was turning red from the harsh contact. My fists shook beside me as tears furiously rolled down my cheeks.

"Why don't you just kill us already?" I screamed when he didn't say anything.

His eyes snapped to my face in confusion. "What the hell are you talking about?" He asked with his eyebrows drawn together.

"Stop playing dumb with me, Weston Marshall," I yelled louder.

"Danny, calm down and lower your voice."

"Why should I? Nobody is home!" I shoved his chest, causing him to stumble back a few steps.

"What the hell?" He said, his deep voice rising. Annoyance was clear on his perfectly sculpted face. "What is your freaking problem?"

"Could you stop lying for once? Just stop it! Do you think I'm stupid? I found out your dirty little secret!"

"I still don't know what the hell you're talking about," Weston yelled back.

"Oh please," I laughed sarcastically. "First, I find weapons that could kill werewolves in your bedroom, Weston! They kill your own kind! I waved it off because you told me you were doing an investigation. I was stupid to believe a petty lie! Let me ask you a few questions on your amazing life, Weston! How is it dating the hunter's daughter? I bet it's superb and magical, but nothing could beat being in the hunting team! That's every werewolf's dream, isn't it?"

Recognition and fear swam in his blue eyes. He adverted eye contact while he found something on the wall remotely distracting. I laughed sarcastically when his jaw clenched and he didn't respond.

"It makes sense now! Werewolves were teaming up with the hunters. Who knew an Alpha would do that? You're clever, Weston. So, here I am. Why don't you kill me now? Get it over with and just shoot me," I crossed my heart with my index finger. "Right here."

He snapped his eyes back to my face before a low growl erupted from his chest. "Never say that again, Danny. I wouldn't dare harm a hair on your body."

"Fuck you," I screamed, a new surge of anger pulsating through me. "You're nothing but a liar! Why else would you be on the hunting team or own those weapons? You want to kill – "

"Shut up," Weston snarled. He tugged at his black hair. "Just shut up, Danny! You think you know everything, but you don't! You think you've got everything figured out, but you're missing a big piece to the story."

My mouth snapped shut on their own accord.

"After you left, I used to run every night to get rid of that fucking annoying pain," Weston sighed. His voice cracked. He sounded utterly broken. He sat down on his bed, looking straight at me. "One night, I shifted back. I was about to head home when I heard the sound of a gun cocking and felt the cold metal of a rifle being pressed to the back of my neck. Once the smell of the wolfs bane surrounded me, I thought I was going to die.

"I turned around and I saw Hayley. She was scared, holding the rifle in her trembling hands. I tried to convince her that I meant no harm, but she didn't believe me of course.

"She almost shot me, but I made the stupid mistake of telling her I'd do anything. I had this idiotic mentality that you would come back to me one day," Weston laughed nervously, scratching the back of his neck. I was happy he wasn't looking at me because my mouth flew open in shock. I was shocked from the story he was currently telling and the statement he just announced.

"Anyways," he continued. "Hayley lowered her gun and asked me to do her one favor. She had a boyfriend who was abusive. She told me she broke up with him. He kept coming to her house when her dad wasn't home to beat the shit out of her. She eventually asked me to be her fake boy friend to scare her ex away. I was a werewolf, so she thought I would be able to protect myself if this guy came after me. I agreed. I mean, I didn't want to die. She knew what I was. Her father was the maker of those weapons. She could nark on me and they would hunt me down. They would've killed the pack.

"After a few encounters with her ex, Hayley seemed to get a little clingy and attached. She'd show up everywhere. She'd call countless times. She came here one night when I didn't reply to any of her calls or texts. Jade answered the door and introduced herself as my sister. I tried telling Hayley that I wasn't interested, but she's a fucking psycho. She threatened to kill Jade if I didn't ask her to be my girl friend.

"I'd never live with myself knowing my sister was dead because of me. I didn't have much options so I reluctantly agreed.

"I didn't want the pack knowing I was dating Hayley. She wasn't special. She didn't matter. I didn't want them to find out she was the hunter's daughter, but Jade made the unambiguous choice of introducing Hayley to the pack.

"After dinner that night, she wanted to have sex. Again, she threatened my whole pack and me. It was practically rape and I was fucking scared. It was hard, but thoughts of you kept flooding my brain and the whole time, I was thinking of you. Just you. I was a pussy. I freaking cried. Could you believe that? I cried when I had sex with somebody that wasn't you.

"After that night, I wanted to kill her. It sounds horrible, I know, but she was crazy and I couldn't stand it any longer. I wanted to turn her in for practically raping me, but Hayley was pretty good at lying and I found out who her father was.

"Her father was the freaking maker of those weapons. She could open her big mouth to him and have my pack and I killed in a matter of seconds. I was scared at first, but I decided to use Hayley as an advantage to investigate.

"I joined the hunting team, but I didn't do any hunting. I got rogues to team up with me and join the team as well. If they decided to attack us, we could attack them before they could reach us. I'll do what it takes to protect my pack and my family."

I had a hard time digesting all of the information. A lot of questions were swarming in my head, but I had a hard time voicing them out. I didn't know which ones to ask first. I didn't even know what to say. The whole room was spinning.

How could I not know that my mate was suffering? It was because I was too busy drowning in self-pity to even realize the pain of my own mate.

I thought Hayley was a normal, average, real, and kind-hearted girl. Looks could be deceiving. She was nothing but a psycho freak.

Weston was right. I thought I knew everything, but I didn't. I assumed the worst from him and I felt so guilty for not having faith in him.

I trusted people I didn't even know instead of trusting the man I loved.

Weston's shoulders were slumped as he stared at his dark carpet with tired eyes. He was stressed and he was in trouble. He couldn't do anything about it. Nothing pained me more to see him so helpless.

I was so stupid and naïve. He did everything to protect us and everyone looked at him negatively because they didn't know the whole story. I mentally slapped myself for believing he was the bad guy too.

After an agonizing long silence, I sighed. He was risking everything for us. I wanted to help him more than anything. "Weston, what do they want?" I whispered.

He still didn't look at me. "Forget it, Danny," He said without room to dwell on it. "Just know that I'm truly sorry for everything."

I gulped. Only now, I chose to believe it. I felt beyond guilty that he had to explain everything just so I could deem that his apology meant something.

Everything clicked into place now. Why he still had our picture by his bed. Why he still looked at me with adoration. Why he spent so much time concerned over my feelings about my mother. Why he kept apologizing.

I assumed he still loved me.

I hoped so.

"I'm sorry, Wes," I whispered, playing with the tips of my brown hair. "I'm sorry for everything. I'm sorry for being an a-hole towards you. I'm sorry for Hayley. I'm sorry for everything and anything."

"We're both at fault," he said. He looked up, finally meeting my eyes.

"Do you still love me?" I blurted, feeling the butterflies flutter furiously in my stomach. I felt like a fifteen year old who's crush just smiled at her.

My heart pounded hard against my rib cage when his blue eyes melted. The answer was clear from the way he stared at me.

"More than anything in the whole damn world," Weston smiled genuinely. "I still lobe you, Daniella Saunders and I've missed you so damn much."

I felt like I was floating when I walked to where he was sitting. I smiled brightly as I stood in between his legs, running my hands through his black hair and resting them on his neck. He wrapped his arms around my waist, pulling me closer to his body. I inhaled his scent deeply, pressing my forehead against his while I got lost in his blue eyes.

"I lobe you too, Dot," I whispered, smirking. "So much that it hurts."

I crashed my lips onto his familiar warm ones.

Chapter 17

NOT EDITED!

The kiss was amazing.

No adjective could describe this kiss.

It sounded cliché, but it was the absolute truth.

It left my toes curling, my taste buds craving, my stomach flipping, my heart racing, my head spinning, and my body tingling. The fire licking in my stomach and the heat that invaded my body were gladly welcomed. It made me realize how much I missed him and his kisses.

Our lips moved in synchronization, molding perfectly together. I could feel his smile against my lips. He kissed me softly and passionately, showing me how much he missed me and how much he loved me. The intensity and the passion in our kiss made my heart burst with happiness.

I suppressed a low moan when I felt him suck on my bottom lip, demanding entrance. I pressed my lips together tightly. He growled as I giggled. It turned into a full out laughter when he tickled my sides. He laughed as he kissed my jaw and left kisses down my neck. When he reached my mark, I felt him smile before he kissed it softly.

He stood up from the bed, grabbing my head. Bringing his lips back to mine, he slipped his tongue into my mouth. I moaned when it came in contact with my own.

My hands tugged at his soft black hair. I was surrounded in his heavenly scent. His every touch was bringing fire to my body. If I could kiss Weston forever, I would.

He rested his forehead against mine when we both ran out of breath. Leaving a trail of heat and goose bumps behind, he ran his hands down my arms and interlocked our fingers. He brought my right hand up to his lips and kissed my palm.

"Gosh, I missed making out with you," Weston groaned.

"Is that all you missed?" I scolded with a fake glare.

"Well, I missed the sex too," Weston teased. He chuckled as I slapped his chest. "I'm kidding, Ells. I missed everything about you."

"You're too cheesy, lover boy," I smiled, patting his cheek lightly.

"Only for you," He winked and groaned again. "I want to show you off, but that psycho bitch is in the way."

"What are we going to do about her?" I sighed, feeling my happiness go down the drain from our reality.

"Hey," Weston reassured, tightening his hold around my waist when he felt me draw back from him. He tilted my chin up with one finger so I could look into his determined blue eyes. "I'll deal with her. I want you. Only you."

"Mine," I whimpered, voicing the thoughts of my wolf.

Weston chuckled. "Don't worry, babe. I'm all yours."

"I like the sound of that."

I closed my eyes as he chuckled and pressed a soft kiss to my forehead.

***

Once again, both packs were cramped in the conference room. There were hushed conversations and friendly greetings as more people filed in. Children were playing games with each other, teens chatted animatedly, women gossiped, and men talked about "men" stuff.

Abigail stood close to Eli. Her eyes were trained to the ground as curious individuals glanced at her. No doubt have they heard the news. Jade and Stacey were offering cookies to the crowd. Charles, Alex, and Dustin stood stiffly in the background, obviously uncomfortable for being on Crescent Pack territory. Jet was deep in conversation with his younger siblings. Beau stood next to me, playing Candy Crush on his iPhone. Jarred and Weston were looking through papers in the corner.

Weston caught me staring at him and a small smile formed on his handsome face. I resisted the urge to pinch him when he linked with me.

'Like what you see?' he asked arrogantly.

'Very much,' I teased, deciding to joke around with him. 'I just want to rip your clothes to pieces and lick my tongue across those finely defined abs.' I choked back a laugh when he turned a slight shade of red, shifting his weight to the other foot. He scratched the back of his neck. 'Too bad that'll only happen in your dreams, Dot.'

Weston and I had been secretly seeing each other behind everyone's back for a week. Sometimes, our friends would get suspicious, but we'd wave it off. They didn't need to know we made out in his room late at night or we'd cuddle and watch a movie.

Every time I saw Hayley, I resisted the urge to shred her face to pieces. Her sweet smile was sickening. When she put her arms or her lips on Weston, I growled inwardly.

Weston reminded me it was all an act and it was going to end soon. He kept contact with Hayley to a minimum and he'd constantly apologize if she so much as held his hand.

'You know what they say. Dreams do come true,' He laughed.

I rolled my eyes. 'If all of your dreams are that illusory, your dreams must never come true. That is sad.'

'Yes it did. I got you.' I felt the blood rush up to my cheeks. A small smile formed on my face.

'Very smooth, lover boy.'

'Stop talking to me,' he joked. 'I'm trying to focus on Alpha duties.'

A very mischievous thought raced through my mind and we all know how much I loved to mess with Weston. I knew exactly what swayed him and what affected him. I smirked.

With the best seductive voice I could muster internally, I linked him.

'Yes, Alpha Weston.'

In my peripheral vision, I saw him stiffen. He was looking at me. I could feel his gaze burning holes in my side. Through the link, I heard him growl lowly.

'You're evil. You're such a tease, Ells,' Weston groaned.

'What? Everyone calls you that. What makes me any different?' I asked innocently.

'Coming from you, it sounds crazy sexy.'

'Whatever. Just remember that although you're an alpha, I'm still your master.'

'Well, I do like my women on top,' Weston joked.

'You are so nasty! Gross! You have a perv –'

"You smell like him again, you know?" Beau said, interrupting me from my conversation with Weston. My heart raced in my chest as he said this. However, my face was set and my lie was already rolling off my tongue smoothly.

"Like who?"

"Don't play stupid with me, Danny," He rolled his eyes and sighed. "I knew you two wouldn't be able to resist each other any longer."

"I don't know what you're talking about," I replied, observing my chipped nail polish indifferently.

"Fine. Don't tell me. I really don't understand why all of a sudden you don't trust me anymore," Beau feigned hurt. I could tell. He was playing the guilt card, but I knew that a tiny bit of him really did feel that way. I gulped, playing with the tips of my brown hair. "When you're ready to tell me, then I'll be there. You don't have to lie to me. I'd hate him, sure, but I would support your decisi – "

"Fine," I huffed, feeling the blush creep up my cheeks. I crossed my arms over my chest, ignoring his penetrating gaze. "We've been seeing each other secretly."

"He's cheating on Hayley?" Beau asked. His eyebrows drew together in confusion. "You're helping him cheat on Hayley?"

"It's a long story," I sighed, looking around me frantically. "I'll explain to you after the meeting. I don't want anybody else to hear."

"Promise?"

"Promise."

After a few more minutes, the meeting finally started.

"Good Evening," Jarred greeted the crowd, causing the hushed whispers to cease. Even the children stopped playing, listening to the Alpha of the Stone Pack. The teenage girls gave him their full attention, obviously attracted to my best friend. "Thank you all for attending our meeting today. We apologize for such short notice, but we have a very important announcement."

From the way Jarred said the last part, we all knew that whatever news was going to be shared wasn't good. Everyone in the crowd watched with fearsome eyes. Their attentions were focused on the two Alphas at the front of the room.

"I will give the floor to Alpha Weston of the Crescent Pack," Jarred announced. "He's truly been on top of his game and found out a lot of information that benefited our packs in many ways."

The crowd clapped. My heart swelled with pride, knowing what my mate did and risked for both packs. He stood at the front with his shoulders squared, smiling gratefully at those who praised his work.

"Thank you, Alpha Jarred," Weston said in a deep voice. I resisted the urge to roll my eyes at the dramatic sighs coming from majority of the young females. "The Stone Pack has a great Alpha. He has done a lot as well. He helped out as much as he could. The effort and dedication he has towards his pack is admirable."

The crowd roared with applause again. I never remembered both packs were this friendly. Jarred and Weston had obviously left high school behind them and started on a new page. It shocked me to see that the two men were ... friends. They no longer butted heads and disagreed on petty things. They were actually praising each other.

"There are no other ways to break the news softly," Weston said with a hint of sadness in his voice. The crowd went dead silent again. Even the representatives wanted to hear what the Alphas had to say. I've been anxiously waiting for some news on the problem at hand. "Therefore, I am just going to announce it as simply as possible."

Gulp.

"Alpha Jarred and I order that all werewolves will lock up and keep careful for the next three days. Keep your families safe. That is all we ask of each one of you. The attack is unfortunately imminent. The representatives will be fighting in three days."

Chapter 18

Not edited

After the announcement, a huge commotion broke in the conference room. The men wanted join this fight too to protect their family. The females were frightened. The teenagers were quiet, but I could tell what they were thinking. They wanted to stay away as much as possible. The little kids really didn't understand what was going on. After all, they were so young.

We, the representatives, were speechless. We didn't know how to respond to the news, but we saw it coming anyways. We knew it was bound to happen. We stood there, trying to regain as much composure as possible in front of the frightened crowd. However, I could feel the fear rolling off of each one of us.

I would be lying if I said I were prepared. I was anything but prepared. Frightened wasn't even the right word to describe what I really felt. My stomach was hurting. My head was pounding. The more I dwelled on the situation, the more reality hit me.

We could be dead any second.

With one shoot of their gun in the right place, we would kiss our lives goodbye.

We had to do this though. The only things motivating us were our family, the ones we loved, and the survival of our packs. We needed to do this. There was no thought of backing down for us.

When Weston and Jarred had finally convinced the men that they were forbidden to fight in combats unless it was deemed necessary, they reassured the crowd that everything was going to be fine. Eventually, the crowd walked out of that conference room frightened nonetheless. Some individuals wished us good luck and thanked us for our bravery.

Little did they know we were shaken in the inside.

After the crowd left, that was when the representatives broke down. We were firing questions at nobody in particular. We were ranting aloud. We were sharing our anxiousness with one other.

I guess it only enhanced the commotion when Weston decided to explain the whole story to the representatives. I reassured him that they would understand and they deserved the right to know what was going on. It took him a couple of minutes to say everything. He told them everything, including the news that we've been seeing each other.

I guess I didn't need to explain to Beau after all.

A blush crept its way up my cheeks when I received shocked gazes from my friends. They turned their heads to study Weston whose eyes were fixated on the marbled tiles. Their mouths hung open and everyone looked absolutely bewildered.

"Oh my gosh," Jade whispered.

Soon, everyone had something to say about it besides Jarred who knew the whole story.

"If I ever see that girl ever again, I will tear her to shreds," Stacey growled.

"What the fuck," Beau muttered, not knowing what else to say.

"Have you found a way to protect us from wolfs bane?" Charles asked urgently.

"I always thought she was a bitch. I never liked her," Jet spat out, crossing his arms over his chest.

"When the hell did everything get so fucked up?" Dustin grunted.

"Psychotic, desperate, disgusting, freaky, slut," Abigail said every word with disgust.

"I don't want Abigail fighting this fight," Eli said eventually. We all stared at him. It was rare to see Eli so serious. If he was this serious, he didn't leave any room for discussion. "She's still ill."

"I'm fine, you buffoon," Abigail snapped. "I'm not even sick anymore. Thank you, Danny, for your amazing healing abilities for the wounded and the sick. Eli, seriously, I'm fine. I could fight. I want to fight."

"Abs," Eli said painfully.

"Dude, bro. Stop hovering over her. You're her mate, not her father," Charles interrupted.

I used to think Charles was a smart guy. It was worse because he wasn't exactly Eli's biggest fan. He was very idiotic for interrupting a conversation between Abigail and Eli especially when Eli was in his serious mode.

"Shut the fuck up," Eli growled, sending a death glare to Charles. "I didn't ask for your opinion."

"What are you going to do about it, huh?" Charles snapped back.

"Stop being so immature," Abigail groaned. "You guys are so freaking annoying."

"He's interrupting a conversation he clearly has no reason to be involved in," Eli complained.

"Bro, I'm just saying you have to respect her decisions," Charles replied.

"Quit fighting," Jarred growled at his Beta. "This is not needed at a time like this."

"Eli, I'm afraid the decision is up to Abigail," Weston sighed, slapping a hand on Eli's back for comfort.

Abigail grabbed Eli's face in between her small hands. She whispered some things that we couldn't hear. When he shook his head, she whispered furiously. She grabbed his hand, before turning to look at us.

"I'm in," Abigail announced. "This is for our packs, for our families, for the ones we love."

Eli didn't say anything. He simply just stared at the ground with his eyebrows drawn together.

"What exactly is the plan?" Jet asked eventually. "Are we just going to walk out in the open and wear signs that read 'shoot me'?"

"You're such a damn pessimist," Jade hissed while Eli smack the back of his head.

"Excuse me for being scared," Jet snapped back.

We were all in the heat of the moment. It was definitely a first time to see everyone bicker or snap at each other. I guess you couldn't blame them if there was an eighty percent chance of dying.

"We all are," I said, looking at everyone straight in the eyes. "But we were chosen as representatives for a reason. We will stand by the sides of our Alphas and Betas no matter what and we will have the strength to support our Alphas and Betas."

Everyone stayed quiet after that. I sighed, before saying, "I'm pretty sure there is a plan."

"Yes, there is," Jarred replied. "Weston made a plan early this morning. It isn't the safest plan, but it's the smartest plan."

"Well, what is it?" Abigail asked.

"You guys might not agree with me," Weston groaned. "But this is the smartest way to do it."

"We ask that you obey what orders you are given," Jarred spoke for both Weston and himself. "If not, you will face the consequences of breaking the representative oath. We would hate to do that to you guys especially since you are the sons and daughters of the representatives before us and have strength and agility that other werewolves weren't so lucky to have. We would also hate to do that because you guys are our friends. It's hard to let friends go. So, don't let this get any harder than it is."

"Right," Weston agreed with a slight frown on his face. "So, if any one of you does not want to fight, please let us know now."

There was a quiet silence. We looked at each other. None of us chose to back out of course. We were stronger than that.

"Good," Jarred said when everyone agreed silently to fight. "Every one of you is vital to both our packs. We thank you for all you do."

"Why do you sound like your saying good bye?" Stacey whispered.

"I'm not saying good bye. I have faith in us," Jarred replied, but even I was unconvinced.

"What's the plan?" Beau asked, looking at Weston.

"Remember how I told you that the rogues were working with me?" Weston begun. Everyone nodded. "Well, here's the plan. The rogues and I are going to be with the hunters when they arrive at our training spot. We will lead the hunters there. We've already convinced them that we saw werewolves in this area.

"As much as you guys will hate to hear this, we are going to try our best to not injure any humans. This is important. If we do harm or kill them, this will give the town reasons to hunt us down. These hunters have families too and people who love them. It may not make any sense to some of you. You're probably wondering why we should spare their lives if they haven't even given us a chance.

"But that is why we are going to convince them that we mean no harm. We're not going straight for violence. Once you start war, it is hard to end it. We refuse to put our packs in that danger.

"We're going to make an agreement to live peacefully amongst them. Therefore, we will lead the hunters into the open field where we will all be standing in our human forms. It is risky. It isn't safe, but it's safer than approaching them in our wolf form.

"If they do try to attack, we have enough rogues to knock the weapons out of each hunter's hands. We have about twenty hunters and fifteen werewolves. If they do shoot, that is where I trust you guys to use your werewolf abilities to move out of the way as quickly as possible. Be alert. Be prepared.

"If they do harm the rogues and you, that is when we attack," Weston finished.

We stared at him with our mouths slightly open. He wanted us to just ... stand there. That is practically signing our death wish right there.

"You want us to just stand there?" Abigail blurted out.

"Yes," Weston sighed. "I knew it would be hard to convince you guys."

"How do you know the rogues won't turn their backs on us?" Charles asked. "After all, nobody should trust a rogue."

"I agree with him on that," Eli added.

"The Alpha rogue is my cousin. A bigger rogue group attacked his pack in Georgia. Out of eighty people, twenty made it out alive," Weston stated reluctantly. We gasped, horrified looks on each of our faces. "They diminished that rogue group and those twenty werewolves have lost everything. They're going to join our pack. They heard about the hunters and they want to help."

"There are no other ways to approach this situation?" Alex piped in.

"We don't have time to think of another solution," Jarred answered tiredly.

"Have you found a way to protect ourselves from the wolfs bane?" Stacey whispered, looking at her feet. Obviously, the memories were still fresh in her head.

"Unfortunately, we cannot do anything about these weapons." Weston tried to keep his voice even, but it trembled at the end. "The only thing to protect us from the wolfs bane is ourselves. So be alert. Be prepared. I trust you every one of you. When you're in doubt, remember why you're fighting in the first place. Good luck ... to all of us."

Chapter 19

It was late when everyone headed to bed or homes to get some rest. However, I doubt that any of us would be sleeping well tonight knowing that the attack was approaching. We couldn't even eat devour our dinner like we usually do.

The silence at the table was sickening. We were all drowning in our own thoughts. It was the first quiet dinner that I had with the Crescent and Stone Pack.

Would we be lucky enough to have another dinner together?

I refused to dwell on the outcome of the problem. The more I thought about it, the more I scared myself. What I should be focused on was the problem itself and how we were going to carry it out.

I couldn't sleep. It felt hot and stuffy in my room. I tossed and turned, causing the blankets and pillows to fall off my bed and onto the floor. After several minutes, I groaned and walked out.

Before I knew it, I came face to face with Weston's door.

Softly knocking on it, I whispered, "Wes, it's me."

"Come in," he said.

I opened his door slowly, inhaling his strong, mouth-watering scent. Worry lines creased my forehead as I saw him sitting on his bed with his head in his hands. I shuffled my feet all the way to him until I sat next to him.

I couldn't find the right words to say. I didn't exactly want to tell him he shouldn't have to worry so much. That wasn't such great advice at the time, especially since I was worried too.

"Hey," I said, playing with his black hair. I wanted to take Weston's mind off this whole problem – even for just a few minutes. "What do you call a fat psychic?"

"What?" He muttered, looking up at me. Under his blue eyes were dark bags. His jet-black hair was messed up, as if his hands been running through them all day. He was still in his clothes from earlier – dark jeans that looked great on him and a button up shirt.

I gave him a small smile. "A four chin teller."

The corners of his lip twitched. He shook his head. "You're lame, babe."

"I'm cooler than you'll ever be," I joked. Weston snorted. When he didn't say anything else, I spoke again. "I know this is such a stupid question to ask, but it never hurts to ask. Are you okay?"

Weston sighed, looking at me. There was a pang in my chest when I saw the broken look on his face. He looked away, staring at the carpet between his legs. "I'm freaking scared," he murmured. "I'm scared that my sister will get hurt once again. I'm scared that the plan won't go well. I'm scared to fail you guys. I'm scared to lose any of you. I'm scared that my mate won't walk out of their alive and it'll be all my fucking fault."

My heart broke.

"Look," I said sternly, grabbing his face in between my hands. "It's okay to be scared, Wes. Just because you're an Alpha, doesn't mean that you have to shove all your emotions aside for business sake. We all make mistakes and we will all stand by you no matter what. I will be okay, I'll make sure of it."

"Promise me, Danny," Weston said seriously, rubbing the small of my back with his warm hand. "That you'll be okay."

"I promise, Weston," I whispered.

"If I don't make it out alive, just know that I love you and I always will," Weston whispered brokenly.

"Don't say that," I gasped. I could feel my eyes water from the way he doubted himself. "Don't you dare say or think that, Weston Marshall."

I studied his face. I traced my index finger down the side of his face, over his cheekbones and down his jaw line. Finally, I touched the scar on his bottom lip lightly. "We'll be fine as long as we're careful," I whispered.

Weston didn't say anything. He just pushed his forehead against mine and stared at me with his intense blue eyes. I shivered as he pressed his lips softly against mine.

He groaned as I bit down on his bottom lip and sucked on it. His hands gripped my hips when I granted him entrance. His tongue danced with my own, causing fireworks to explode on my taste buds.

The warmth from his body was addicting. His scent was mouth watering. I needed to get closer to him.

There was too much space between us.

There were too many clothing between us.

Curse my perverted mine, but I wanted more.

I brought one of my legs to the other side of him, straddling his waist. He grunted as I pressed our bodies flushed against each other. I tangled my hands in his black hair as his hands wandered down to cup my butt cheeks.

I smirked against his lips when I felt his excitement. My fingers fumbled with the top buttons of his shirt. Once the first few were unbuttoned, he pulled off his shirt and threw it to the ground. He wasted no time in crashing his lips back on mine.

I still couldn't get enough.

I wanted him.

My mark was burning.

There was a throb between my legs.

Weston ran his hands down my bare legs. I shivered. He moved his lips along my jaw line and down the column of my neck, sucking and biting. He nibbled on my ear lobe before whispering, "Your scent is driving me crazy." I moaned softly as he sucked on my mark. I threw my head back and involuntarily, I grinded my hips against his.

He growled, gripping my hips tighter and turning us around so my back was flat against the soft mattress. He hovered above me, pressing his lips against mine.

Every kiss with Weston was amazing. Every kiss felt ten times better than the last. He showed passion, hunger, want, longing, love, and many more emotions with every brush of his lips.

I felt him shiver as I ran my hands down his muscular abdomen. His warm hands roamed up my shirt. He was taking his damn time. He was teasing me. Groaning, I pulled my shirt off my body and threw it on the floor.

Weston looked at me with swollen lips. His blue eyes had darkened with lust and love. He stared into my eyes. "God, I'm the luckiest man in the world," he groaned.

I laughed.

"Gosh, I love that laugh," He muttered, nuzzling my neck before crashing his lips onto mine once again. He pulled away once more. "Danny, if I'm pushing you, tell me. I don't want to risk losing you again."

My heart shattered into a million pieces. He thought he lost me the first time, but that was entirely my fault. I let him believe that he lost me. It wasn't his fault.

Tonight, I was going to prove to him that it wasn't him.

Tonight, I was going to show him how much I missed and love him.

Tonight, I'm going to show him I'm all his.

Tonight, I was going to apologize for my mistakes.

Tonight, I was going to make it up to him.

I seductively bit my lip and motioned an index finger to come closer to me. I didn't know where this sudden burst of confidence came from, but I think Weston liked it. He leaned in. I scratched his muscular back with my nails as I whispered some things that are better left unsaid.

Let's just say I was telling him exactly what I wanted him to do to me.

He pulled away when I finished whispering. His dark eyes widened and if it were possible, they darkened some more. He growled before pressing his lips on mine hungrily.

Soon, all of our clothes were on the ground and he pressed his lips to my mark once again.

"I love you, Weston," I whispered breathlessly.

"I love you too, Danny, so much," He mumbled against my neck before entering.

That night was amazing. It was ten times better than the first time we made love. For one night, our minds were off all our problems.

All that I could think about was Weston.

Needs proofreading *

<h1 style="text-align:center">Chapter 20</h1>

M y hands trembled as I climbed out of my Land Rover. I'm sure the news had reached my mom, Darren, and Kelly, but I knew I still had to explain it to them myself. I also knew how they would react.

They weren't going to like the news very much.

Weston noticed me stall. "Ells," he said, grabbing my trembling hands. He kissed my palms. "You'll do fine. Your family has always been understanding. Do you want me to come in with you?"

I shook my head. "I think I should do this on my own," I said. "It's a family issue."

"Okay, if you need me, I'll be in the car."

I nodded, pecking his lips. Walking towards the double doors, I started spacing out. I was forgetting what exactly I was going to tell them.

We all knew how it felt to tell our families harsh news. Either it be a failing grade, a boy friend or girl friend you weren't allowed to date, cracking your mother's favorite glass bowl. In this case, I was practically telling them I might die and I wanted to see them before that happened.

I didn't want Weston to come with me inside. Many things could go wrong. Darren would probably rip his head off for letting me fight in this fight. My mother would probably do the same. Weston would cause a riot in my house and that was something I shouldn't have to worry about at a time like this.

"Hey guys, I'm here," I yelled out when I finally opened the doors.

I heard footsteps running down the stairs hurriedly. I looked up and saw Kelly, her blonde hair bouncing as she ran down the stairs. She looked at me and pointed a finger.

"You are in trouble, missy," She scolded, folding her arms across her chest. "Your brother is so not happy with you. Please tell me you refused to join this fight."

I looked down at my feet, shaking my head slowly. "Oh dear lord," Kelly gasped. "Please tell me you're kidding."

"I'm – " I began, but an intimidating male voice interrupted me.

"Daniella Jean," My older brother called out. I flinched at his unhappy tone. He stomped down the stairs and stood next to Kelly. He folded his arms across his chest. "Explain now."

That's what I liked about Darren. He always made me explain before he scolded me right away. He heard me out before deciding whether he should scold me, wave it off, or reassure me he wouldn't tell our parents.

"There's not much to say. I'm sure you heard about what is going to happen tomorrow," I shrugged. "I'm going to stand with the packs."

"No," Darren finally said, making it seem like there was no room for discussion.

"Darren," I sighed. "I have to do this. I'm doing this for you guys."

"Danny, mom is injured badly because of me. If I allowed you to walk into danger, I will not forgive myself if you were harmed. I cannot afford to watch you suffer."

"And I will not forgive myself if I didn't try," I snapped back. "Darren, whether you allow me to or not, I will stand there and I will do this for our family. There is no way you could change my mind."

His shoulders slumped tiredly, before he sighed heavily. "You're not going to," He said through clenched teeth. His hands balled up into fists. "I'll take your place, Danny! I don't want you risking life. You're so young."

"You're two years older than me!" I screamed at him, trying to reason with him. "Darren, you've fought for our family so many times. It's my turn. You stay here and take care of mom." I walked up to him and threw my arms around my brother's shoulders. "I'll be fine," I whispered. "I promise. You guys are my motivation."

As I hugged him, he was stiff. I could tell he was caught in an internal battle. After a few more reassuring words, Darren's shoulders slumped and he wrapped his arms around me. "I trust you, Danny," Darren said. "But I'm sorry. I can't approve of this."

"I know," I smiled, pulling back. "I knew you wouldn't approve and I know you will never approve."

"If you don't come out of there alive," His voice trembled. "I don't know what I will do."

"I will come out of there alive," I whispered. "If I don't, just know you are the reason I'm this tough today. I cannot express my gratitude. I'm so blessed that I have you in my life. You taught me so much. I love you, big brother."

"I love you too, little sister," he replied solemnly.

"Hold your head up high and smile," I recited the speech that Darren always told me when I was younger. "Stand up tall and remain strong. You are strong."

Although it wasn't funny, Darren chuckled and ruffled my hair. "You too, Danny."

"I've always admired your bravery," Kelly sighed and hugged me tightly. "Please be careful. You're like the younger sister I've never had. I can't imagine life without you."

"Kells, you're like the older sister I've never had," I smiled. "Take care of Darren. I'm glad he has you. He's so busy worrying about everyone else and at the end of the day, you're the one holding your arms wide open for him. Thank you for everything you have done for this family."

After a few more words with my brother and his wife, I headed up to my mother's room. Darren told me she had heard the news and she wasn't happy about it. My hands were clammy as I turned the knob and entered her room.

She was doing so much better. Her skin had her natural glow back. Her eyes didn't droop so much. She didn't look as sick as the last time.

When she saw me, she dropped the remote of the television. She stared at me with broken eyes. Before she even said anything, her shoulders started shaking as she sobbed into her hands.

"Mom," I whispered. I sat by her on the bed, hesitant.

We could all agree on one thing. It was hard to see your mother cry. It broke your heart. You didn't know what to do and before you knew it, you were crying with them too.

My tears streamed down my face as I slung an arm across her shoulder. "Mom," I said once again.

"Danny, you are not going out there," She cried. "I will not let my baby get hurt!"

"Mom, plea –"

"You will listen to me, understand?" She scolded, gripping my arms in her hands. "Please don't this to me."

"I'm not doing this to intentionally hurt you, mom. I'm doing this for you guys. I'm fighting for my family, for my pack, for everything that is right."

"This is not right! You could be dead in a second!"

"I know."

"You know? So why are you going to do it?"

"I have to," I whispered, feeling so small under my mom's angered eyes.

"You don't have to! We'll all be fine if you just avoid the fight."

"Mom, one thing you've taught me was to never run away from my problems. I refuse to do that now. I will not bail on my friends."

"They'll understand! They have to!" My mom's sobs grew louder, causing a tight pain in my chest.

"You have to understand, mom," I sighed. "Please. I have to do this."

I sat there with my arms wrapped around my mother's small frame. I cried as she sobbed into my shoulder, clutching me closer to her. Of course, nothing could convince her.

"I have to protect my baby," She bawled.

"Mom, I'm at that age where it's my responsibility to take care of you. It's my turn."

My mom kept demanding that I stay here with her. She kept scolding me. In the end, she was angry with me. However, she told me that she loved me and that I had better come home alive.

It was them who gave me the motivation to stay alive. They were the reasons – along with Weston and my friends – that I promised myself to walk out of there alive.

I just hope luck will be on my side tomorrow.

As I descended down the stairs, I saw Beau coming up. He gave me a small smile, ruffling my hair. "Hey, cous," He said with an overly cheery tone.

Beau was always good at hiding his true emotions, but I was good at figuring him out. Dancing in his hazel eyes were fear. His fingers tapped against his leg rapidly.

"We'll be fine," I reassured, eyeing his fingers.

"Yeah, we will," Beau chuckled nervously. "After all, we are Wrodes. The Wrodes always make it out alive."

I knew he didn't want to talk about it. Beau was more of a thinker than a talker. Therefore, I just smiled and pinched his cheek.

When I finally sat in the leather passenger seat of my Land Rover, I sighed heavily. Weston observed me with calculating eyes before he interlocked his fingers with my own.

"How was it?" he asked.

"Horrible," I groaned. "I feel bad for doing this to them."

"I'm sorry," he said genuinely. "If you don't want to do this, just tell me. I would understand."

I stroked his face with his thumb. "I refuse to back down," I whispered. "I'm doing this for all the right reasons."

As I stared at Weston, I couldn't help but think of the worst case scenarios. What if I lost him? I heard mates go through depression when they lose their other half. I knew I wouldn't be able to cope with it.

I chose to ignore it and focus of the present. We had to enjoy every precious minute in life while we had it. We all take advantage of time. We never do realize how short life is until it's over.

I closed my eyes and pecked his lips.

"I love you, Weston."

"I love you too, Danny."

Chapter 21

The representatives stood in a single filed line, stretched across the green field. We stood about half a foot apart, stiff and restless. The only sounds that could be heard were the shuffling of our feet and the rustling of leaves.

The cold September air bit at my skin, making it much more uncomfortable. I was paranoid. Every time I heard the rustling of leaves, I would snap my eyes to the area Weston had informed us where they'd be coming from.

My heart was racing furiously. I'd constantly wipe my clammy palms on my sweater. My eyes were constantly open and alert. I kept shifting my weight from one foot to the other.

All of us kept staring at each other, silently wishing the other good luck. I stared at every one of them with gratitude. They all played big roles in my life and had given me so much to remember.

I may not be as close to Charles, Alex, and Dustin currently. It saddened me to think that we used to be inseparable, but they let pack rivalries get in the way of everyone's friendship. Nonetheless, I was thankful that they watched out for me the very first few months I moved to Huntstown. They protected me from a ruthless Weston.

Stacey's sapphire eyes were panicked. I remembered that very same look approximately fifteen months earlier when she was chained to the wall suffering countless injuries. She had gone through a lot, especially with her mate. I admired her for the strength and maturity she had to get back on her two feet and live life without wallowing in self-pity. She was one of my best friends – almost my sister. She was loud, girly, and was really good at peer mediation. Every girl needed a friend like that and I was lucky to have her in my life.

Jet was stoic, hiding his emotions very well. It seemed like just yesterday when Eli and him raced to my table my first day at our high school. They were the dynamic duo and Jet was the clumsy and awkward comedian. Although he was mean at times, I admired him for his straight forwardness and honesty.

Elliot stood protectively next to his mate, arms crossed over his chest. Eli was a class clown, happy going, and down to earth man. Although he was Beta, he treated us all with respect. He may seem like a ditz at first glance, but he was actually very smart. I remember when he would vent to me about Abigail. I remember his jokes and the way he'd get excited over the smallest things. He was one to appreciate the smallest things in life.

Abigail was the very first person to inform me about the Crescent Pack and their arrogance. I'd always tease her about being mated to one of them, but that joke always back fired on me. She had a hard time leaving Charles, but she was in love with Eli. She was always the bubbly one in our group of female friends (Abigail, me, Jade, and Stacey) and she was the weirdest out of all of us. It was hard not to laugh when you were around her.

I remember Jade was the first person I met at our high school. She was part of the unofficial welcoming committee. She was kindhearted, shy, and logical. She would always remind us to think of the consequences before doing what we thought of doing. She was the older sister in the group. She was mature for her age. She always cared for other people even if she didn't know them. I admired her for artistic skills behind the camera lens and the way she was friendly towards everyone she met.

My cousin, Beau, was someone I owed a whole lot too. Not only did he teach me majority about Healers, he took time off his schedule just so he could support me over here. He didn't even need to stand here with us today, but he did. Beau was a great man with great ambitions. I remember when he'd tell me the lamest jokes when I was down or take me out to coffee when our training was over. He treated me like his little sister. He watched over me and protected me. Although Beau seemed like the perfect person with the perfect life, he was broken in the inside. His mom committed suicide a week after his father passed away from a terrible car accident. Although this traumatic event happened in his life, he searched for his mate. He would recite one of his favorite quotes. "It is better to have loved and lost than to never have loved at all." He will find his mate one day.

My best friend, Jarred, who was more like a brother to me than a friend. He deserved the best for everything great he has done in his life. I remember the very first time I met him. It always brought an amused smile on my face as I thought of the lame pick up lines he tried to use on me. He stood up in front of me when Weston was being a jerk. He told me the truth instead of sugar coating things. When I left, he made sure we stayed in touch. He drove down just to cheer me up when I felt my heart breaking to a million pieces. I told him everything and he told me a lot as well. He was a genuinely happy guy, but the people with the biggest smiles have the saddest stories. He never got along with his father or his mother. They always wanted him to be the perfect child with a planned life. Eventually, Jarred strayed away from them and hasn't talked to them for two years. It was hard on him. I promised myself I would never leave him like he has never left me.

And finally, Weston Marshall – my soul mate. He wasn't here at the moment, but my mind strayed to him and I wondered if he was doing fine. It has definitely been a bumpy road for us. Then again, what relationship is perfect? We were far from perfect and that's the way I liked it. He'd been a jerk the first time I met him, but he became the man I loved. After all, what lasts won't always come easy. There were many memories with him. The arguments we had taught us lessons and strengthened our relationship. We had inside jokes that nobody else would understand. His kisses and his embraces never failed to sway me. He was amazing and I was damn lucky to have him. He risked everything for everyone today and I couldn't be more proud of him. He was injured both emotionally and physically because of me, but he never abandoned me. He frustrated me so many times and was a constant annoying bee, but I loved everything about him. I probably sound like an infatuated teenager right now. Sorry, I'm a hopeless romantic. I knew there were going to be many more bumps on the road, but I promised myself we will fix them and I will not run away like the last time. He meant too much to me to lose.

As I stood there, antsy, I thought back to my family too. It was hard to know that they were probably going crazy right now, worrying about me. It was harder when I didn't know if I'd see them after this. I loved them and I couldn't wish for a better family. They gave me things that I didn't deserve. They molded me into the person I am today. This is the least I could do for all they have done for me.

'Guys, get ready,' I heard Weston in my mind. 'We're almost there.'

I gulped, clenching my trembling hands into small fists by my side. With one glance at everyone, we shot each other panicked looks. I could hear their frightened voices in my head, wishing each other good luck. We did not dare say goodbye to each other. We had a hard time.

'Ells,' Weston linked, but only to me this time. 'I'm sorry for everything once again. If anything bad shall happen – '

'Wes, don't,' I replied solemnly.

'No, Danny, I want you to know. If anything bad shall happen, just know I'm sorry I failed to protect you. You're the best thing that has ever happened in my life. Thank you for being you. I want you to know that. It sounds like something from a corny teen chick flick, but it's the truth. I don't think I'll ever get tired of saying this, but I love you.'

'Wes, we'll make it out alive,' I reassured. 'I have faith in us. Thank you for risking everything for us and doing everything you do. You're an amazing alpha and an amazing mate. I couldn't wish for better. I love you too, Dot. Never forget that.'

I heard heavy footsteps and quiet muttering. It was easy to pick up when you had enhanced werewolf abilities. Once their footsteps grew louder, I knew the others could hear it too.

They stiffened, shuffling closer to each other involuntarily. I could practically hear everyone gulp nervously. I could feel the panic rolling off them in waves.

No doubt was I frightened as well.

'We're near,' Weston warned. 'We'll be out in the clearing in less than ten seconds.'

My breath hitched and my blood ran cold when a string of thirty hunters followed behind Weston out onto the open field. I could smell werewolves lingering amongst the group. I could even pick them out. I watched every one of them with calculated eyes, prepared for the first shot. They stood in a cluttered group, holding their weapons in their dirty hands.

They were obviously surprised. They weren't expecting us to show up here. In fact, Weston had told them that they were just crossing this land and they weren't going to encounter us for another mile.

They cocked their guns and aimed their rifles at us. We crouched, growling at them as a warning. The rogues growled too, snatching the weapons out of each hunter's hand with inhuman speed. Hunters groaned and screamed when they realized that their fellow "hunting pals" were really wolves. The shot of a gun echoed in the empty field.

My eyes widened, observing the scene in front of me. A human hunter groaned in pain, hopping on one foot. I let out a relief breath to see that he accidently shot himself on the foot whilst grabbing his weapon back from a fiery red head. Once the rogues grabbed every weapon from their hands, the hunters shrunk back and were prepared to run.

However, Henry held up his hand and ordered, "Stay. We did not come here to run. If you run, they will chase you like dogs do." We growled at him, but he glared at us with hate.

"What the hell is going on?" Another hunter asked, retreating from a growling blonde-haired woman.

Weston walked out onto the open field. He stood beside Jarred who positioned himself in front of us.

"Weston?" Henry's eyes widened. "Son, what are you doing?"

"I'm Alpha Weston of the Crescent Pack," Weston growled, crossing his arms across his chest. "Looks like you guys weren't so smart after all."

"Kids?" Ron gasped, pointing a finger at Beau and me. I rolled my eyes.

"Looks like you can't trust anybody," Henry sneered.

"We're not looking for danger," Jarred said calmly.

One hunter scoffed, glaring at all of us. "Yeah right," He spat. "You're animals."

"We're humans," Weston stated. "We're just supernatural."

The rogues had moved to go join us. In the middle of our groups was a big space. It was quiet as we stared each other down. Finally, Weston spoke again.

"We won't harm you," He said, ignoring the angry shouts from the hunters. "We just want to make an agreement."

"An agreement?" Henry laughed. "Ha! That's hilarious, boy! Why would we want to make an agreement with dogs?"

"What have we done to you?" Jarred snarled. The wolves agreed with him, growling at the hunters.

"You've killed and injured our citizens," A hunter cried.

"We've killed or harmed them because they harmed us first," Eli yelled. "We were using self defense."

"By using your vicious animal side?" Another hunter scoffed.

"You were using weapons that could kill us," Charles replied. "We've done nothing. We didn't even start whatever war we are fighting. You humans have started this and I have to say, you people are more ruthless than us 'dogs' are."

The hunters shouted nasty replies to that one. At every comment, we'd shout back at them. It was more of a debate than actual fighting.

"Enough," Weston growled at all of us. It was so loud and intimidating that the hunters stopped too. Soon, they started their banter again.

"Stop," Henry ordered calmly. He smiled menacingly at Weston. "Now, what agreement would you like to have?"

"Get rid of the weapons. We will not harm humans. It's as easy as that. The weapons are the real problem here," Weston stated.

"How do we know you will keep your end of the deal?" Henry barked. The hunters agreed. He didn't give Weston a chance to reply. "That's right, you won't. You've lied to us once and we were fools to have trusted you. So why should we trust you again?"

"It –" Weston was cut off when Henry took a gun out of his coat pocket. Soon after, the other hunters followed suit.

My eyes widened. Well, we didn't expect that. We crouched down, growling at the brutal weapons in their hands.

"You didn't expect that, huh?" Henry smirked. "We knew there was something fishy about these new hunters. We had to be careful just in case."

'How the fuck did I miss that?' Weston linked us, walking backwards a bit. 'I'm sorry I failed you guys.'

There were a thousand thoughts swarming in my head. I was too young to die. I promised my family that I would come back alive. My friends had families they were waiting for too. My life was over –

"Daddy," A female yelled.

At the sound of the familiar voice, a growl rippled in my chest. Her presence angered my wolf more. I wasn't the only one angry. The other wolves growled.

"Hayley," Henry said, lowering his gun when Hayley stood in front of us. "What are you doing here?"

"Daddy, do not hurt them," Hayley pleaded, placing her small hand on Weston's bicep. Weston flinched away. My growl was low and menacing.

Hayley watched him with wide eyes, but waved it off. "They've done nothing wrong."

She wasn't such a psycho freak after all. However, I still did not trust her. Although our new found dislike for this lady, we kept our mouths shut.

Hayley's statement caused her father to laugh. He lowered his gun and so did the other hunters. "Hayley, honey, I know you're in love with Weston," Henry informed. "But they're nothing but vicious wolves."

"I know," she muttered, scuffling her feet.

"You know?" Henry asked with anger. "You chose them over your own father? Hayley, move, this is going to get a little bit messy."

"No, dad," Hayley said sternly, looking at her father with her big brown eyes. "You promised to stop killing werewolves even if you didn't find what you were looking for. Whatever happened to that? You only want one thing. I know they've betrayed you, but maybe they could help."

"You're right, Hay. Hunters lower down your weapons," Henry gave in at his daughter's words after a ten tense minutes of silence. His eyes were hard to read. "Weston, I know you know what I'm looking for –"

"No," Weston snapped harshly, eyes blazing with anger. "Absolutely not. There is no way in hell that's going to happen."

The question that has been killing me was finally brought to the table. What was so important and so valuable that Weston did not want to hand over to the hunters? If he gave it now, this could end peacefully. I knew Weston had it in his possession because he didn't say, "I don't have it." Instead, he refused to give it up.

"Weston, please," Henry's voice pleaded with hurt. He ran his hand through his hair. "Do you have a Healer amongst you?" He then looked at all of us. "If any of you are Healers or know of any, please help my wife. She's a werewolf and she's been suffering an illness for over two years now. She will die soon."

What the hell was going on?

Chapter 22

S itting in Henry's old SUV was beyond awkward.

Henry thumped his fingers on the black steering wheel, humming to an old tune. I steadied my eyes on the gravel road in front of us while picking on the thread of the faded red seat covers. Ron sat quietly in the middle of Weston and Beau in the back seat.

"So," Ron chuckled nervously. He looked ridiculously tiny adjacent to Beau and Weston. "You guys won't attack us, right?"

"I thought we've established that," Beau snapped, obviously annoyed.

"Okay," Ron squeaked, drawing in a shaky breath. "My mom would definitely ban me from hunting."

"You're thirty-one and you still live with your mother?" Weston asked, shaking his head. "And she still tells you what to do?"

"I love my mom," Ron defended. "We watch Oprah together."

Approximately one hour earlier *

"Weston, please," Henry's voice pleaded with hurt. He ran his hand through his hair. "Do you have a Healer amongst you?" He then looked at all of us. "If any of you are Healers or know of any, please help my wife. She's a werewolf and she's been suffering an illness for over two years now. She will die soon."

What the hell was going on?

Once the words fell out of his mouth, I glanced at Beau. He was staring at me with his eyebrows drawn together in confusion. There were a lot of questions I wanted to ask, but so little time to do so.

I'm beyond confused.

Hayley told me her parents were divorced. Was that one big lie? Was that her psychotic side speaking? If her mother were a werewolf, wouldn't she be one too? Even if her father was a pure human, the offspring was bound to be a werewolf just as long as one of her parents carried werewolf blood.

Why did Henry possess such weapons if his wife was a werewolf? Wasn't he afraid that she'd get hurt? Was that the reason she was ill? From being around wolfs bane so much? Wasn't she angry with him for possessing those weapons?

Weston was wrong to make the decision without asking me first. I was fully aware he knew exactly what Henry was asking even before he brought it up today. Weston knew I was capable of healing a sickness just as long as it was a werewolf illness.

Illnesses such as cancer, HIV, and other diseases were incurable. Healers could only heal what illnesses were passed down in werewolves.

"No," Weston said again, shaking his head furiously. "I will not put her in danger."

"She's your mate, isn't she?" Henry asked after a few seconds of quite thinking. His eyes lit up while he dropped his gun fully. "Please, Weston, I'm begging you. You know what it's like to have a mate – a soul mate. You know you'd hate to see her on the verge of dying."

Henry's voice cracked at the end while a frown fell upon his face. I could tell he was suppressing his tears and trying to keep his composure. However, the more he spoke about it, the more we knew he was breaking.

I couldn't respond at first. It was too hard. I was too shocked to even speak a word. I could tell the others were just as confused as I was. It was silent in my head. I couldn't hear their voices.

Henry looked at every one of us with pleading eyes. When his eyes rested on me for a fraction of a second, my heart stopped in my chest. Should I help him? Was he lying? What if he kills me after I've helped him? Would he? Does he dislike every werewolf besides his wife?

"I know I've done a lot of bad things," Henry started. "But wouldn't you stop at nothing to help the one you loved? I know you wouldn't believe me when I say my wife is a werewolf because I own and create such vile weapons. I tried so hard looking for a Healer once my wife explained how they worked. Therefore, one day, I decided to visit a werewolf pack off the coast of Michigan. They attacked me. That's the reason for my scar. After that day, I've made weapons to protect myself."

"But that doesn't explain the reason why you kill werewolves for fun," Eli spat disgustingly. "Your wife is a werewolf and you killed werewolves with no remorse!"

"I know," Henry sighed. "After I talked to a few more werewolves, I started getting frustrated. I knew they were lying when they said no Healers exist in the world today. My frustration led to killing. I regret it. I don't expect you to understand. Please help me. I've only come across one Healer, but she couldn't help. She only healed disheartening emotions. I swear to you that I stopped killing werewolves after that one moment."

"You guys attacked us twice," Eli cried, pointing to Abigail. Abigail shrank back from the unwanted attention. "You stabbed my mate!"

"I don't know If you've noticed, but we tried talking to you first. However, once you guys smelled the wolfs bane, you automatically growled at us. You would circle us or bare your canines. We were scared," Henry stated as if it was obvious. "So we would attack. We apologize. But you guys never gave us a chance."

'Is this true?' I asked the pack through the mind link. I wouldn't know because I haven't been present during these attacks.

It was quite before Jade replied.

'Now that I've thought about it, they have tried to tell us something. Our minds would focus on the weapons, not the people,' Jade gasped. 'Now I feel horrible.'

'It's okay, Jade,' I replied when nobody spoke up. 'I would have reacted the same way if I saw deadly weapons.'

'I'm going to help him,' I linked quietly when Weston still refused Henry's offer. Henry even gave his gun to one of the Rogues and showed empty pockets. Henry then ordered the other hunters to give up their weapons.

'What?' Everyone responded.

'No,' Weston growled. 'Fuck no, Danny.'

'Why not?' I snapped angrily. 'It was wrong of you to make my own decision.'

'I'm your mate.'

'Exactly. You're my mate, not me.'

'No.'

'Weston, this could be over if I helped his wife.'

'Why would you want to help her?'

'Henry was the one who did wrong things, not his wife.'

Silence. 'How do you know they wouldn't hurt you?'

'I don't.'

'Then you're not going.'

'You can't stop me.'

'Please don't do this to me, Danny,' Weston pleaded brokenly. 'What if they're lying? What if they hurt you? What if everything goes wrong?'

'Life's full of risks, Weston,' I sighed. 'I can't waste such a beautiful talent.'

'They'll kill you if you don't succeed in curing his wife,' Weston said lowly, almost as if it pained him to say the words. 'I won't allow you to walk into that.'

'I'll take care of it,' I replied hastily before putting my block up. There were too many voices in my head. If I tried to let them see my point, that would take the entire night. The only quiet one was Beau, who nodded his head at me in agreement.

I stepped up, ignoring Weston's warning glares.

"Henry," I cleared my throat awkwardly. His eyes snapped to me. I saw realization swimming in his brown eyes. Everyone watched me silently. Beau stepped beside me, blocking my view of Weston. "Is your wife's sickness a pure werewolf illness?"

"Yes," he whispered, eyeing me if I were God – which was very awkward. "Her wolf is very sick. We're not sure what illness it is. We've tried everything to heal her, but nothing worked."

Werewolf illnesses were hard to pin down. They were so much alike, it was hard to distinguish them. Being a Healer, all you needed to do was mutter words while waving your hands over the patient's entire body.

"Ells – "Weston called quietly.

"My cousin, Beau and I will be able to help you," I suggested, ignoring Weston. "But we'll only do it on several conditions."

"D, this is not a good idea," Jarred whispered.

"Anything. I'll do anything," Henry replied eagerly.

"Your hunters will stay here under the watchful eyes of my friends," I ordered confidently, motioning my hand towards the werewolves. "They must submit every weapon to us they possess as of right now and empty their pockets. Your men will be kept in our conference room until I am sure you will keep your word. You may take Ron with you if that makes you feel slightly safer. You, too, must prove that you have no weapons on you or in your car. My friends will destroy the weapons that they have collected today."

"I'm not asking you to completely destroy the wolfs bane weapons and plants. I'm afraid that it's too late for that. Your men will probably have one hidden under their beds at home for safekeeping. However, I shall warn you. A healing is a gift from the ancient Healers. They watch you. If you do come after us and try to extinguish our beings after the healing is done, your men and their families will suffer treacherous consequences that are better left unsaid." There were several gasps from both the hunters and the werewolves. It was true. If a healing was done under terms and conditions, anything that is agreed upon must be followed. It was a taboo to break promises if something as big as healing was being done.

"You will stop selling or creating those weapons," I continued. "Finally, I want werewolves to live peacefully amongst you. We will not kill or harm you if you do not kill or harm us. It's as simple as that. Once you agree to these terms, there is no turning back. Break one of these agreements and you shall live with the consequences. Believe my words. A person once went psychotic and committed suicide because he broke a promise," I said seriously. Healing was serious.

Henry looked at his hunters, before they nodded slowly. They had fear in their eyes, but they looked slightly calmer than they did before. I guess it was because I decided to help them.

"We were only in this group to help Julie," One hunter said, taking his cap off. "She's my sister."

"I'm pretty sure we all agree," A female hunter nodded her head. "We never meant to harm you and if you help Julie, we will know your intentions are good. We will leave you alone."

"After you recite your promise, you swear your lives to the Ancients. We cannot control what happens next unless a new agreement was made. This is a serious matter," Beau said. When the hunters nodded, Beau continued. "Raise your right hand and say, 'We agree to the terms and conditions of this agreement.'"

An amazing thing happened next. The hunters stood in a single filed line – including Hayley. They raised their right hands, reciting the words. Goosebumps covered my skin. This was my very first agreement. I could feel the Ancient Healers watching.

"Great, let's get this show on the road," I grinned. The wolves have started patting down the hunters before heading towards the house.

"I'm coming with you," Weston stated, leaving no room for discussion. He gripped my hand and walked next to me as we followed Henry and Ron into the forest, towards Henry's car. I simply shrugged, letting Weston tag along.

Henry's car was an old SUV with sunspots on its faded red paint. Jarred and Eli had inspected his car before heading back towards the pack house. Henry smiled before we all piled into the spacious Ford Bronco.

Inside, a radio sat on the dashboard. The car's radio was long gone. A pine scented air freshener hung from the rearview mirror. His seatbelts looked dangerously weak. I sat in the passenger seat, my right leg bouncing up and down.

Sitting in Henry's old SUV was beyond awkward.

Henry thumped his fingers on the black steering wheel, humming to an old tune. I steadied my eyes on the gravel road in front of us while picking on the thread of the faded red seat covers. Ron sat quietly in the middle of Weston and Beau in the back seat.

"So," Ron chuckled nervously. He looked ridiculously tiny adjacent to Beau and Weston. "You guys won't attack us, right?"

"I thought we've established that," Beau snapped, obviously annoyed.

"Okay," Ron squeaked, drawing in a shaky breath. "My mom would definitely ban me from hunting."

"You're thirty-one and you still live with your mother?" Weston asked, shaking his head. "And she still tells you what to do?"

"I love my mom," Ron defended. "We watch Oprah together."

My eyes widened in surprise. I turned around to face Ron and saw that Weston and Beau were staring at him with a "what the hell" expression. Ron stared at his feet, chuckling nervously.

"We won't hurt you, man," Weston sighed, patting his back. "We made an agreement."

"Right," Ron said unconvinced with a nervous smile on his face.

"Thank you," Henry whispered. My eyes snapped to him. His expression was relaxed. It was as if a huge weight was lifted off his shoulders.

I couldn't blame him though. If Weston was suffering from an illness and I couldn't do anything about it, I'd stop at nothing to find help or assistance. Like Henry, I knew how it felt to love someone and I didn't want to know how it felt to lose that person.

Weston meant a lot to me.

I knew Julie meant a lot to Henry.

"You're welcome," I smiled, feeling good with myself. "I wouldn't want to lose my soul mate either."

"I met Julie two years after I've divorced my first wife – Hayley's mom. The first time I laid eyes on her, I instantly fell in love. Along with Hayley, she's my happiness and she's my world," Henry's voice was filled with so much love and happiness. I wondered if I sounded like that when I spoke about Weston.

His statement answered a lot of questions. Hayley was a human. Henry remarried. It made perfect sense now.

"So Hayley likes her step mom?" I asked, surprised that I was actually conversing with a man that almost killed me today.

"She's happy if I'm happy," Henry shrugged. "Hayley suffered a whole lot when her mother and I had the divorce. Next thing you know, she was suffering from depression and she constantly felt lonely. Docs prescribed her medicine. After the Healer I told you about healed her, she convinced us that she was okay without the meds. I didn't know the healing of emotions would last that long."

There was another answer to my question.

I felt a sudden sympathy for Hayley before it quickly went away. That was the reason why she was so clingy and attached to Weston. She was looking for something that was absent in her own home.

I wanted to tell Henry that Hayley had lied when she said she was fine. She wasn't. Healing of emotions doesn't last that long. They were only temporary – like a high from a drug. However, I didn't want to give Henry more to worry about at the moment. It wasn't my place to tell him. It was Hayley's obligation to tell her father the truth.

Julie was pretty with long, honey blonde hair that framed her heart shaped face. Her eyes were a dark green. She was terribly skinny for a werewolf. Her translucent skin was nowhere being healthy at all. There was a limp to her walk. I cringed when she lay down on the bed with struggle.

"Danny, you've got this," Beau encouraged when Weston collected Henry's weapons. "Just remember what you've learned."

"Beau, I wouldn't be here if it weren't for you," I smiled, giving my cousin a big hug.

"I think I found her," Beau whispered in my ear. It took me a second to realize what he was saying.

"What?" I exclaimed. Sudden happiness wrapped itself around my heart. I couldn't stop the huge smile that stretched across my face. I punched Beau's arm. "You will have to explain later!"

I bent down next to Julie who had a small smile on her face. "God bless you, Danny," she whispered breathlessly. "I'm blessed that God has led me to Henry. He found you."

I smiled. "Julie, he loves you a lot."

"Ah," Julie laughed tiredly. "That's the beauty of mates. You know what true love is. Anyone who has found it should not let it go."

Her statement caused me to look back at my rough past with Weston. I shouldn't have let him go like that. I would regret that decision for the rest of my life.

I was lucky I found him.

I was lucky I still had him.

I've learned that if you were lucky enough to get it, then you should cherish and keep it.

"That is so very true," I chuckled, before placing my hands on Julie's head. "I need you to relax and close your eyes. Think of happy thoughts and positive outcomes. Don't think too hard of the situation at hand. Think of what would happen if you're healthy again. Imagine sky diving with Henry or shopping with Hayley."

"Hilatu illateru sikeru. Hilatu illateru sikeru. Hilatu illateru sikeru ..."

The words rolled off my tongue. I was so much better at healing that I could do it with my eyes opened. I smiled when I saw that it was working.

Julie's color was coming back. Her lips and cheeks were regaining its normal rosy color. The dark bags under her eyes receded a little bit. She looked healthier and stronger.

"You could open your eyes now," I whispered after the whole process.

Julie opened her eyes without struggle. She sat up slowly without moaning in pain. Her eyes were wide before she threw her skinny arms around me. "I don't know what to say. I feel better. I literally felt my illness go away. It felt like water rinsing off dirt from my hands," She gushed. Even her voice sounded better. "Thank you, Danny. I mean it."

"Okay, I did enough to heal the illness, but you will still have a fever. Eat the right food so it could restore the nutrients in your body. Rest up. You should be fine in no time," I ordered. Julie nodded her head happily.

"You're amazing! I feel so much better! I feel so alive! I haven't felt like this in a long time! Thank you so, so, so much! I cannot express my gratitude enough!"

I laughed as Julie continued her happy banter. Soon, Henry joined us in the living room. Along with Julie, they kept praising me on my work. Every time they would finish their statement, they would shout out their appreciation.

These times made me proud to be a Healer. We were a rare form of werewolf that was supposed to be extinct centuries ago. Slowly, we were proving that are intentions were not bad. We were made to help, not to cause danger.

Slowly, the werewolves were also proving they didn't want to cause harm to humanity.

"I owe you guys a lot," Henry said after profusely apologizing for everything he did. We didn't quite trust him yet or accept his apology. "So, can we call a truce?"

I smiled at Weston who looked at Henry's outstretched hand, before shaking it. "Truce," Weston smiled.

***

"Did I tell you how lucky I am to have a sexy Healer as a mate?" Weston mumbled, nuzzling my neck.

I laughed, ruffling his black hair. "I guess luck was on both our sides."

Weston smiled, crashing his warm lips on mine. The moment felt right, kissing my mate under the stars on our spot on the porch steps. Then again, it always felt right with Weston.

And it always will be.

Chapter 23

S ix years later

"Hey cutie," I cooed to the one year old in Jade's arms. She looked up at me with adorable crystal blue eyes. I held out my hands. "Come to Auntie Danny."

"Come on, honey," Jade encouraged her daughter. "She won't hurt you."

Baby Jasmine looked away, burying her face in the crook of her mother's neck. Jade sighed, bouncing up and down. I just chuckled, tickling Jasmine's small back.

"She's too attached to Jarred and I," Jade rolled her eyes. "The only other person she'd go to is Weston."

"She's too cute," I cooed.

"Just like her father," Jarred said cockily, slinging his arm around Jade. He took Jasmine in his hands and smiled at her. "Did Aunt Danny scare you again? She is scary, huh?"

I smacked Jarred's shoulder. He poked his tongue out at me before taking Jasmine into the kitchen to feed her. Jade rolled her eyes once more.

"Jarred is spoiling her way too much," Jade said with a slight smile on her face.

"Well, that is his very first princess," I laughed.

"Danny," A female voice yelled. My eyes widened when Abigail came running into the dining room. She wrapped her arms around me. It was somewhat hard to hug her back with the round belly she was sporting. "Congrats, college grad! You could finally be a teacher."

"Thanks," I replied, smiling at the accomplishment.

"Abs," Eli entered the room with a panicked expression. "You're squishing my baby!"

"Shush," Abigail pulled away, rubbing her belly. "He's my baby too."

"It's going to be a girl," Eli argued.

"It'll be a boy. I want a boy first," Abigail said angrily. "So Jasmine and him could be together."

"Jasmine is going to be two years older than our baby," Eli cried. "Women are so confu – "

"Eli," Warren called from the living room. "You're missing the football game, man. Where have you been?"

Before Abigail could say anything, Eli dashed off into the room with the other men. A few seconds later, Stacey joined us in the kitchen. We all stared at the living room door when the men screamed and shouted. We simply shook our heads.

"Hey pretty ladies," Stacey greeted. "How are my best friends?"

"Lacking sleep," Jade replied. "Be warned, Abs. Once your baby is born, she or he will keep you awake."

We laughed, knowing how much Abigail cherished her sleep. "I'll let Eli take care of the night shift," Abigail joked. She turned to Stacey with waggling eyebrows. "How was your first anniversary with your husband?"

Stacey blushed. She winked. "I'm afraid that is confidential information." We laughed.

Abigail and Eli were the first to get married. They got married two years ago. Months after, Jade and Jarred vowed their love to each other. Last year, Stacey and Warren got married. Even Beau married his spunky, red head mate about a year and a half ago.

Beau moved back to his home with his mate. I decided to stay here. Occasionally, I'd drive down to visit Beau. I was extremely ecstatic that he found himself a mate. She was everything Beau was looking for.

"What about you?" Abigail scolded, pointing her finger at me. "Woman, you're already twenty-five. You found Weston about nine years ago. He needs to fertilize the soil or glue a ring to your finger. What the hell are you guys waiting for?"

I blushed, shuffling my feet. Everyone was married or had kids. Weston and I were in a serious relationship, but we never talked about getting married or having kids. We went with the flow. Usually, it didn't bother me. However, now that I was twenty-five and all my friends were starting a lifelong relationship and family, I wanted it too.

I didn't know how to respond to Abigail's question. I didn't have to. At that moment, I was lucky a familiar brown haired, brown-eyed boy ran in. My four-year-old nephew threw his arms around my waist.

"Auntie Danny," Kyle exclaimed, smiling up at me.

"Hey monster," I said, ruffling his hair.

"Where's Uncle Weston?" He asked curiously after hugging Abigail, Stacey, and Jade.

"He's in the living room watching football with the guys."

"Cool," he yelled, running into the living space.

My mom came into the kitchen carrying a two year old in her arms. I took my nephew in my arms, cuddling him close to me. His curly brown hair peeked out of his small baseball cap. "How's my little Keegan?"

"Kyle took ball. All gone," Keegan said with a pout. His speech was improving.

"Auntie Danny will buy you another one," I promised, kissing his cheek.

"Hey mom," I greeted.

"Hey Danny," My mother responded, flinging her arms around my shoulders. "Congratulations on your graduation!"

I laughed. "Thanks mom. Where are Darren and Kelly?"

"Still at work," My mom sighed. "I swear they work too hard. They'll be here in a few minutes."

"Good," Abigail groaned. "I am starving."

"You're always starving," Stacey teased, poking her belly. "Pregnancy is scary."

"Everything is scary to you," Jade replied.

My phone notification went off. I pulled my phone out of my pocket, reading the text message.

'Hey Danny, sorry couldn't make it today. Congrats on your graduation! I'm still in California with the girl friend. Her parents are so creepy. They own porcelain dolls. I'll make it up to you. –Jet'

I smiled, chuckling at Jet's text message. Just three months ago, Jet had found his mate. Ever since then, he has become a huge softie. He agreed to meet her parents this month. He stated that she was very different from her creepy family.

When everyone got here, we sat together at the long table in the pack dining room. It was loud as usual. This time, Jasmine was crying. Kyle and Keegan were making airplane noises at the end of the table. Everyone talked here and there. Eli and Abigail continued their usual banter.

"Congratulations to our graduate," Jade called out, toasting. "Danny, you will make a great teacher."

There were cheers and claps. I smiled at my friends and my family. It was nice being surrounded by the ones you loved. I wished it would stay like this forever.

Weston hand squeezed mine and he smiled at me. "Congrats, babe," He whispered. "You'd be one hell of a sexy teacher."

I rolled my eyes, but the small smile on my face lingered. "Since you're a teacher now, could I ask you something?" He asked it loud enough for everyone to hear. The silence that followed was suspicious. Their excited faces were mischievous.

"Go for it," I replied, shrugging.

Weston smiled, kissing my cheek. My mouth dropped open when Weston dropped down onto one knee, digging in his pocket for a velvet black box. I laughed when Weston scratched the back of his neck before opening the jewelry case.

I felt happiness and love burst inside of me. Before I knew it, tears of joy rolled down my cheeks rapidly. I giggled, wiping the tears with the sleeve of my shirt.

Weston opened the box. Inside was a simple, elegant, and beautiful diamond ring. His eyes were boring into my own. I swear I would never get tired of his beautiful, blue eyes. His other hand held my face.

"Daniella Saunders, I lobe you so very much," He said loud and clear. "I want to spend my whole life with you. You've invaded my heart. I know. That sounded very cheesy. So, will you marry me?"

I didn't even have to think twice.

"Yes!"

www.ingramcontent.com/pod-product-compliance
Lightning Source LLC
Chambersburg PA
CBHW070356200726
48294CB00003B/939